Chapters Of Life

Luke's Return
Book Three

(Book 17 in the series Chapters Of Life)

By
Ed Harris

Published by
The Bancroft Press

This edition first published in 2019
ISBN: 978-0-244-17632-7

www.edharris.co.uk

Chapters Of Life comprises 14 separate books in total, covering the years 1962-1968 of teenage Bromyard life.

The set also
includes the following volumes:

Chapters Of Life - The excluded Chapters - Books 10-14
Chapters that were omitted from the original 9 Chapters series for various reasons.

Plus
Chapters of Life - The Return - Books 15-22
Luke's return to Bromyard

While the first 14 books in the Chapters Of Life series dealt with Luke's life up until 1968, these following books (Luke's Return) deal with events post 1984, when Luke returned to Bromyard.

Whereas the books dealing with events up to 1968 were taken from the daily diaries of 4 local Bromyard girls, and are based upon actual events described within them, these that deal with post 1984 events are based upon nothing more than pure fiction, only using the framework of the earlier works to tie them into the location, so as to create a continuation of Luke's various adventures.

Chapters Of Life

Luke's Return
Book Three

Chapter 1

The cemetery in Bromyard seemed to have mellowed with age since his last visit. So too, had Hazel and Crista's grave.

Luke placed the flowers in the weather- beaten vase, straightened up the leaning angel, then sat down next to the headstone.

Reading the inscription, Luke dug his fingers through the cool grass, feeling the moist earth below. His beloved pair were only six foot away from him, but lost forever, or until he joined them at the end of his earthly life.

" Hi there baby. I hope that you and little Crista is keepin well. I still love you as much as ever and miss you like crazy."

Luke swallowed hard, trying to fight back the tears of emotion that were welling up inside him, rapidly blinking the tears away.

After tidying up the edges of the grave, Luke kissed the headstone and walked away without going to look at either Rosie's or Julie's graves.

Luke walked up through the town and into the car park where he had left the car. Quite a few people were about now, gazing in the various shop windows or simply standing around talking.

Those that recognised Luke, spoke, before passing on, and Luke stood on the corner of Davidson's old shop, smoking and gazing at nothing in particular.

A loud hooting came from the horn of a battered Morris Traveller that had pulled up at his feet and Luke recognised the grinning face of Derrick peering out at him through the grubby side window.

Yanking the passenger door open, Luke hopped in as they took off with a judder. Derrick's hand clasped Luke's tightly as he swerved around the corner into the Tenbury Road.

" Christ, Lou. I thought it was you. I couldn't believe my eyes. It's bloody great to see you again, mate."

" Yeh. You too, Derr."

" How long have you been back?"

" Only just got here, mate. Been down the cemetery, seein to the family, like."

" Yeh? There's a few of us down there now. Come on, I'm takin you home. Mo will never believe it unless she sees you for herself."

" You two still together, then?"

" Yeh. Well, more or less, you know how it is, mate. Wot about you?"

" Oh. I'm about all over the place."

" Haha. Ain't changed then by the sounds of it, has you?"

" Naw. Never will, neither."

Mo smiled warmly as Luke entered behind Derrick and hurried forward. Luke grabbed her and kissed her parted lips, grinning as he let her go, seeing her embarrassment.

" S'matter, babe, thought you always wanted me to kiss you?"

" Oh, Lou. God. You haven't changed at all, has he Derr?"

" Nope. That's what I said to him earlier."

Mo grinned as she eyed him up and down.

" You seem well enough on, whatever, anyway."

" Oh yeh."

" Coffee, Lou?"

" Cheers, black, no sugar."

" God."

" S'okay, babe. Sugar makes me too energetic."

" God help us, then.   What about milk? No, on second thoughts, don't answer that."

" Tell you wot, Mo. You're still a little cracker though, ain't she, Derr?"

" Oh, yeh. keeps me hard at it, she does."

" Oh, be quiet. Oh, hello love. Lou, this is Debbie, our little girl."

" Whoo. Hi baby."

" Hello."

The young girl moved on and took the kettle. After refilling it, she plugged it in, switched it on and started to get out the mugs for them all.

" Everyone for coffee?"

They all replied in the affirmative, and Luke watched her as she moved about the room. Debbie had her Mother's hair and colouring. Her figure was slimmer, but he could see Mo in her in twenty years time,
She gazed at him over her shoulder.

" Milk. Sugar?"

" No thanks, Debs. Just black."

Mo grinned.

" Debbie's 22 now, Lou. You never knew her, did you?"

" Nope. I was long gone before she was hatched. Hayley was the only one you had then. Last time I was here I never caught up with you."

" Oh yes. Nasty business, that."

" Yeh. Oh, thanks Debs."

" And, I was not, hatched."

" Sorry."

" You aren't Lou Brown, are you?"

" Yup. Fraid so, girl."

" Hmm."

" Now, Debbie. You shoot off and do whatever you do, will you?"

" Oh, Mum. You are a meanie."

" Well. I expect your Dad and Lou want to talk."

" Yes. I bet they do, too."

With a little laugh, Debbie carried her drink out without a backward glance.

" Cheeky madam."

" Yeh. Just like her Mum used to be."

" Lou. You never knew me that well."

" No. I didn't, did I?"

" Hey, you two. Can anyone join in, or is it private. You'll stay for dinner, won't you, Lou?"

" Well."

Mo smiled.

" Oh, come on, Lou. Stay here for a few days, with us. Hayley's married now and there's only us and Debbie. We've a spare room all kitted out for you. Nice pinks and flowery curtains."

" You sure, Mo?"

" Of course we are. God. It's years since we've seen you. It's going to take ages to get through all of the gossip."

" Yeh. Okay. I'll go and get me motor though."

" Where is it?"

" In the top car park, where Angel Place used to be."

"Hah, your old house, Lou. A bit different there now. Tell you wot, I'll whip you down there, mate."

" Naw. S'okay. I'll hoof it, enjoy the scenery. I could do with the exercise."

" You looks fit enough to me, Lou?"

" Yeh. All the work I don't do."

" " Yeh. I can believe that, too."

" How's things with you, anyway, mate?"

" Oh. Not too bad, Lou. We make out, you knows how it is?"

" Yeh. You workin?"

" Yeh. Part time. Fitting central heating boilers. I'm based in Worcester. Get all over the bloody place too, sometimes."

" Nice.."

" Yeh, can be."

" Oi. You two. Come on. Whenever Derr starts talking about the old days, I have to virtually threaten to hit him, and, where you're the topic, Lou, nothing will shift him."

" S'okay Mo, we ain't got there, yet."

" Oh. God. That's a bad sign, then. He gets a funny look in his eye where you're concerned."

" Oh yeh? Well, I ain't queer, honest."

" Oh, Lou. You haven't changed, have you. Still the same."

" Worse, baby, believe me."

Luke excused himself after almost an hour and, after promising to be back by 1.00pm for dinner, strolled down the hill, heading towards the town.
Luke could feel some tension in the air between Derrrick and Mo, but did not enquire as he watched the 2 of them.
Yes, Luke thought, all was not well there.

There were new estates everywhere now, and Luke stopped for a few minutes as he came to the playing fields gate at the end of York Road, leaning on it to scan one of his old stamping grounds.

" Hi, bovver boy."
" Oh,. Hi Debs. You followin me?"
" Do I really look that desperate?"
" Cheers, girl."

Luke grinned at her as she leant on the gate next to him.

" Changed a bit, since your day, I expect, hasn't it?"
" My day? Cheeky git."
" I meant, dear ole Lou, all the new houses and that."
" Oh. yeh. Bloody hundreds of them, now."
" Oh well, Lou. I can call you Lou, can't I?"
 " Well, yeh. It is me name."
" Good. Better than calling you, Mr Brown."
" Up yours."
" See. It makes you feel your age."
" I'll kick your arse in a minute, girl."
" Oh. Violent as ever, I see?"
" You goin to friggin well slag me off all the time, or wot?"

" Okay. Sorry. Truce?"

They shook hands solemnly, and Luke grinned at her bubbly humour as they walked together through the long grass towards The Ballhurst and the town.

" Are you coming back for dinner?"
" Yeh."
" And tea?"
" Yeh."
" Uhu."
" Wot's that mean?"
" Oh. I was just thinking that you lot are probably going to be up all night yakking about the old days. Think I'll stay up and listen, should be quite fun."
" Yeh. Educational, too."
" Don't know about that. Bikes, girls, drink, fighting, sex, girls and, yet, more girls. You did know Mum then, didn't you?"
" Oh yeh. I knew little Mo alright."
" Why are you smirking like that?"
" I ain't."
" Yes you are. I'll tell her."
" You would, too, wouldn't you?"
" Yes. Unless, you make sure that I'm allowed to sit in on your reminiscences tonight, that is."

While Luke waited for Debbie to get her few things from the shops, he sat on the low wall surrounding the car park at the top of the town.

As she came back, Debbie smiled and waved her carrier bags at him.

" Finished. Where's your car, then?"

" Over there."

She looked around.

" Where?"

" Up the top, by the loo's."

" Oh. Come on then. Show me."

Luke followed her as she walked through the parked cars and, as she walked straight past the gleaming bulk of the white XJS, he sat on the bonnet, waiting for her to turn around.

He eyes widened as she came back.

" Is that really yours?"

" Yup."

" My God. Wowee. Boy Oh boy. What a car. Is it really, honestly, yours?"

" Yeh. Told you it was. C'mon, get your arse inside, or we'll be late for nosh."

"You didn't nick it, did you, Lou?"

"Nah, you cheeky mare, course I didn't."

Luke opened the passenger door and Debbie slid slowly across the pale leather seats as they both grinned broadly.

" Oh. What a car, Lou?"
" Yeh. Ain't bad, is it, baby? I'd sooner have the XJ6 though, more class to it."
" Oh yes. Undoubtedly. How can you say that, Lou. This car is so, so fab. More class, than this?"

Her arm swept around the car in an expansive gesture.

" Oh, come on. Take me home, James."

Derrick's and Mo's reactions were the same after Luke had drawn the gleaming sports car up behind their little Morris Traveller. They sat in it, walked around it touched it and stroked it before they were satisfied that it was real.

" Useful little shopper that, Lou?"

Derrick's voice was full of envy and Luke grinned.

" Yeh. Give it a spin sometime, mate. if you wants?"

" God. No thanks. I'd be scared in case I scratched it."

" S'only a poxy motor, mate."

" Only a motor? Not to me it ain't, Lou. I won't ask what you does for a living, but you seem to be doing well at it?"

" Yeh, can't complain, mate."

His tone made them all laugh, and they soon settled down in the kitchen for their meal.

Luke spent the afternoon lazing in front of the fire listening to Debbie's records. She had some Abba ones and kept playing ' Move On' for them.

Mo laughed at Luke's expression.

" It's her latest ' in' record. Last month it was 'Oh Well' by Fleetwood Mac. Next month it will probably be the Stones or something."

Derrick had to go and visit his ill Mother, and Luke told him to take the Jaguar, but he declined and drove off down the hill in the Traveller as Luke gazed out of the window after him. Luke grinned inwardly as he remembered the old headmistress at Bredenbury girls school all those years ago and her Morris Traveller. Miss Wendy Poulter. Luke wondered where she was now.

Was she still stuck in that tunnel at Symonds Yat? He shuddered inwardly as he recalled it all, that really was a mystery, all that had happened to them both whilst in that tunnel.

Luke also quickly realised that when Derrick 'Visited His Mother', it was a euphanism for something quite different. Mo did not elaborate too much, merely informing Luke that Derrick had been seeing another woman for years now.

Mo spoke to Luke quietly as the music played, and Debbie tried blatantly to eavesdrop , even turning the sound down at one stage.

" Debbie. Will you please stop being so nosy."
" I'm not."
" Yes you are. Lou, she's terrible, isn't she?"
" Aw. I dunno. Let her listen if she wants. Bet we'll soon have her blushin before long though."

Debbie turned her back on them hurriedly, her tone off-hand as she selected another record.

" Huh. I doubt if it's really that bad, anyway."

Her Mother laughed.

" You'll never know, will you?"

" I will."

" How?"

" Because, dear Mumsie, I'm going to listen."

" We'll wait until you go out tonight then."

" I'm staying in tonight."

" What?"

" You heard. I thought that I'd give it a miss for once."

" Good God. Whatever's the matter with you?"

" Nothing. It gets boring being stuck in a pub all night."

" What about the dance?"

" Well. That's the same. Same old faces, same old music."

" Well. I've never heard you say that before. You still can't listen anyway."

" Oh yes I can."

" Debbie. You heard me."

" Lou said that I could."

Mo's face swung to his, her eyes enquiring, many questions shining from them.

Luke raised his shoulders and grinned.

" Yeh. I said it was okay, providin that you agreed, too, mind."

" I see."

" Mo, if you don't want her to, I'll change me mind?"

No. You're right. She'll soon be blushing, I bet."

When their tea was over and all of the things had been washed and dried, they all settled down in the front room in front of the fire. Debbie offered to make them all coffee while Derrick sorted out all of his old records, putting on Sonny and Cher ' I Got You Babe'

" Hey, Lou. remember this one. You and Tom used to crack us all up doin this."

" Oh yeh. I remember it."

" Great stuff, Lou. The Tamla groups. Ronettes. Martha and the Vandella's."

" Okay, Dad. Don't blow a fuse. "

Debbie handed the drinks round and smiled at Luke as she raised her eyebrows.

" He does get carried away a bit."

Derrick laughed.

" I do? Hell. You should have seen Lou if you thought I does. Hey, Lou. Remember that day in the

Doors when you were all over, who was it? That French bit, Tom's cousin, weren't she? Anyway, remember, Jane turned the juke box up so loud that you couldn't hear anything, but you and her, you never even heard it, did you? God. What was her name?"

" Chantal."

" Oh yeh. That's it. Chantal. And in the back bar of the Queens, too. Ha."

" Yeh. Okay, mate."

" What happened to her?"

" Went back to France, didn't she."

" There was a whisper that she was up the duff?"

" Yeh?"

" Yeh, Lou. Hey, remember old Tramp?"

Mo laughed.

" Oh, yeh, Lou. She was a right laugh. Remember that day in the caff when you hit her?"

" I didn't actually hit her."

" Okay, you shoved her against the wall. And Emily stormed off in a huff?"

Derrick grinned, his mouth wide.

" Whoo. Yeh. Emily. My God. What a piece she was. God, I remembers her well. Jeeesus."

Mo glared daggers at her Husband.

" Oh, yeh. That's right. I might have guessed you'd remember her, too."

" Okay, love. She was a bit, well, you know, special, wasn't she, Lou?"

" Oh yeh."

Mo sniffed.

" I knew there was somethin goin on between you right from the start."

" Oh yeh?"

" Yeh, Lou. Come on, it's over twenty years ago now, when did it really start between you and Em?"

Debbie had sank to her knees onto the mat in front of the fire, her eyes wide above her coffee cup as she followed all that was said.

Derrick tossed a lighted smoke over to Luke, who caught it deftly and smiled at Debbie.

Putting down her cup, she put her head to one side and poked her tongue out at Luke as Derrick laughed, his eyes on Luke.

" Hey, Lou. Remember that Rachel, the farmers Daughter?"

Mo broke in.

" It was Elizabeth, her Mother, I think, who was the attraction there. Am I right, Lou, dear?"

Luke laughed and nodded.

" Yeh. Let's just say that I was interested in livestock, shall we?"

Even Debbie laughed at this as Derrick continued to chuckle.

"Ha, yeh, Lou. I remembers Tramp pullin them knickers from your pocket in the Doors, and that Rachael lookin like doomsday had hit her."

Mo giggled.

"Yes, cos they was her Mother's knickers, all posh and shiny silk. Haha."

Luke grinned as he shook his head, remembering the incident in all its clarity.
Debbie looked hastily into her coffee mug and blushed as Luke winked at her, grinning broadly.

The evening passed into night as they re lived their old memories. Again and again, the talk touched on Emily and, as casually as he could, Luke asked.

" Seen anythin of her lately, mate?"
" Nope. Nor her Brother or Sisters, neither. Jackie's still around somewhere. Why, you still interested in Emily?"
" Course he is, Love. Them two were inseparable. Why they never got married I'll never know."
" Yes, love. But it was over twenty years ago now."
" Doesn't make any difference, Derr, does it?"

As her two parents went on, Debbie rose and whispered in Luke's ear, her warm breath making Luke quiver.

" Want another coffee?"
" Cheers, baby."

She gathered up the cups and went into the kitchen, leaving the door open so that she could still hear. She was soon back, and the talk turned towards bikes. Derrick was still peeved because he was never allowed one of his own, but told the stories of Luke's escapades to them, making Debbie's eyes grow wider at each story.

" Oh, Dad. It can't all be true?"

" It is, love. Hey, Lou. What about that Bikers Chapter that you were in, in Worcester? Heard a lot about you from there, who was it, Spot, wasn't it? Come on, refresh my memory?"

So Luke recounted some of his exploits to them, leaving out those that contained some of the grislier details.

Mo went and prepared them some sandwiches for a late supper, while Debbie saw to the coffee supplies.

Luke went to the toilet and came back to the strains of The Beach Boys singing ' God Only Knows'.

He grinned at Derrick as he regained his seat.

" Didn't know you liked this one, Derr?"

" Yeh, well. It has a certain memory, if you see what I means?"

Derrick bent his head to Luke and whispered a name in his ear.

Luke looked up and they both laughed loudly together.

" I never knew that, Derr?"

Mo's voice reached them from the kitchen.

" And I don't even want to know what that was all about, Lou Brown."

" It weren't me, baby."

" No. It never was, was it, Lou?"

" Hey. How's the old Moorhen doin, anyone know?"

" Yeh. He's dead, Lou."

" Naw. Is he?"

" Yeh. A few years ago."

" Pity. He weren't a bad sort really, was Maurice."

" Nope. You certainly had some mileage out of him."

" How?"

" Well, besides practically runnin the place, weren't you also official bed tester for his female staff. If they performed okay, then they got the job?"

Debbie almost dropped the tray in her haste to get her head down and Derrick grinned at her reddening cheeks.

" Hey, Lou. Remember when you almost stripped that one across the top of the counter. God. I bet she was ever sore afterwards. Ha. All we could see was you pumping away at her. Mind, she seemed to be groping you well."

Debbie flew back out into the kitchen, almost knocking her Mother over in her haste. Derrick roared and explained it to his Wife, who grinned.

" It serves her right then. Nosy little madam."

As they settled down once more, Debbie reappeared and sat in front of the fire, studiously ignoring them all as she stared into the dancing flames.

They talked until well into the early hours as the old music played and, when Luke finally did hit the sack, was asleep within minutes, smiling as he recalled Debbie's, still averted, eyes as they all rose from their seats. Well. She had wanted to listen, hadn't she?

The next day Luke was up early and went downstairs to find Mo preparing breakfast for him.

She smiled warmly at him and pecked his cheek.

" Derr's gone out to see some copper pipe, or something."

" Bent stuff?"

" Haha. No. It's all legal, honest."

" Yeh. Still have the local paper round here?"

" Yeh. But there's never much in it. It ain't the Bromyard Record anymore, pretty useless all in all. Last weeks is over there, help yourself."

" Cheers Mo. I just wanted to see wot was about. Sure brought it all back last night, didn't it, babe?"

" It certainly did, Lou. Only seems like yesterday."

" Yeh. "

" Do you really miss Emily that much?"

" How much?"

" Oh. Come on, Lou. I noticed, even if no one else did. All of those little half questions about her."

" Jeez. I'm glad you ain't the CID."

" Ha. I'd have you, mate. believe me. Oh. Hello love."

" Lo, Mum."

" Hi, babe."

" Hi, Lou."

Debbie drifted over to the coffee pot, filled a cup, then drifted out again without another word.

Mo grinned.

" Talkative, isn't she?"

" Yeh. Perhaps we disillusioned her last night?"

" I've never known her so quiet. We'll have to try that again tonight?"

" Yeh. I'll bring you up to date."

" That will be fun, I bet. You'll stay for the weekend at least, won't you, Lou?"

" Well.I was goin up the old man's place. Yeh, Okay, go on then, I'll stay, cheers. May as well. I'll give you somethin for my keep."

" Don't you even think of it. You're our friend, Lou."

" I'll remember that, Mo. I'll be back by tea time. Okay?"

" Okay. Come and go as you please, Lou. This is your home for as long as you want it."

" Cheers, baby."

Rising, Luke kissed her on her full on her lips once more and, as she blushed, went out, quietly laughing to himself.

Chapter 2

Drawing to halt outside his Father's house up the Bannut-tree estate, Luke finished his smoke, still deep in thought about many things as he tapped the steering wheel with his fingers, finally sighing and crossing to the back door.

He collected his post from El, and sat at the front room table as he flicked through the many envelopes that lay before him.

El placed a hot cup of coffee before him on a flowery-patterned round plastic coaster table and grinned.

"That should keep you going for a while, Lou."
"Yeh, cheers, El."

Coming to an A5-sized one, Luke frowned as he saw his London Solicitor's name and address stamped at the top.

Sighing deeply, Luke carefully tore it open, wondering what was up now.

Luke's eyes scanned the contents, then turned to the other letter that lay inside the envelope. Luke reading again, this time more slowly as he digested the contents.

Dear Mr Brown,
Please find enclosed a communication from the late Miss Julie Stevens.

This was passed on to us after several months of searching for your whereabouts by Miss Steven's solicitors.

Miss Steven's has left her entire estate to you, including her house and its contents.

Besides this, she has left you the contents her bank account, which stood at £29.876 at the time of her death.

After all payments, the balance of £29,478 is yours.

If you could contact us at your earliest convenience, we can then start the legal process of transferring the property to you and depositing the money into your account.

Yours faithfully,
J Foster.

So, Luke thought quietly to himself, what did Julie want to 'communicate' to him?

She had left him her house and almost £30.000. Luke was amazed at the size of this, as he did not realise that Julie had saved this sort of money, having told Luke that she had 'A bit put by'.

The outside of the other envelope simply said, 'To Mr Luke Brown'.

Opening it, Luke took a gulp of coffee as he started reading.

My dearest Lou,

as this letter was to be released after my death, then you already know that I am no longer with you, for whatever reason (unless, of course, that you are already dead, then we have a problem).

Everything that I own, Lou, I leave to you.

You are the only one that I have ever loved, the only one that I have ever wanted, the only one that has kept me going all of these years.

My heart has always been yours, my darling, Lou.

Perhaps we are already married by now, though somehow I doubt that.

Please enjoy my little gift to you, Lou, and, always take care, please.

I will be waiting for you, Lou, when it's your turn to arrive at the Gates Of Heaven.

With all of my heart and soul, I love you so very much, my darling, Lou.

Yours forever and a day,
Julie
xxxxxxxx

Sitting back in his chair, Luke simply handed the letter over to El, as she came bustling into the room, stopping dead in her tracks as she saw the sombre expression on Luke's face.

As she read, El sank into a chair next to Luke at the table, and, glancing at him, re read the contents before setting it down on the table silently.

Luke pushed the letter from his solicitor over to her, and, again, El read the contents without uttering a single word.

Sighing deeply, she placed the letter next to the other and shook her head.

"Christ, Lou, nearly thirty grand, and her house. God, that girl worshipped you, didn't she?"

"Yeh, and look how I repaid her, El, I caused her to fuckin well kill someone else and herself. I am such a cunt, El."

"No, Lou. None of this is your fault."

"Like fuck it ain't, El."

Al came into the room just then, and stood staring at them both.

Before he could speak, El held up the two letters and, taking them, Luke's Father began to read through them.

He, too, seated himself at the table, his eyes burning deeply into Luke's.

"Boy, I don't know wot to fuckin-well say. I really don't."

El squeezed Luke's hand as she turned to Al.

"Lou blames himself for the deaths, Al."

"That's a load of bollocks, Lou. It was her choice. Julie snapped, no fault of yours. Remember, she was always a bit, well, like that, weren't she?"

Luke shook his head.

"Because of me and the way I treated her."

"No, Lou, She was like it right from the start, from when she was attacked, remember?"

"Yeh, I remember. But if I hadn't fucked her around, they would both still be here. Instead, they ain't, and all cos of me."

Al bumped his chair closer to Luke, laying his massive arm around his distraught Son's shoulder, his voice soft and caring.

"Lou, believe me, boy. None of this is down to you, honest. We can't control other people's lives, and we can only influence them to a certain, small degree. Julie just snapped, Lou, not because of you, but because of her make up, the way that she was inside. She was highly strung, emotionally, and, well, was allus flyin off the deep end, you knows that more than anyone.. There was nothin that you could have done to stop this happenin, Lou. Just enjoy wot she left you and remember her, remember the happy times that you had, and go and see her grave occasionally. That's all any of us can do, Lou."

Luke sighed deeply and grasped his Fathers fingers as he squeezed.

"Yeh. Yeh, you're right, I knows that. But. Ah, yeh, fuck it. You does talk some sense sometimes, old Son. Thanks, I appreciates it."

[Over the course of the next week, Luke contacted his solicitors and set the wheels in motion.

He asked El to go into Julie's old house and select anything that she wanted and to arrange the disposal of the rest of her belongings, and, within a further 2 weeks, the property was up for sale.

6 weeks later, the house had been sold, and Luke's bank balance was inflated even more than it had been previously.]

He was rich, but alone, and Luke felt that he would always be so, for everything that he touched, on a friendship level, seemed to wither and die.

Luke knew full-well that it was due solely to his attitude towards life and women, the feeling that he always needed to move on and sample something new. He did this knowing that the end result would always be the same, and that, once the chase had ended, he would rapidly become fed up with the hum-drum of life, having already felt it with Maire. He simply had to always be on the move, it was his nature.

For the next hour or so he sat in his Father's and El's front room, bringing them more or less up to date on events in his life, leaving them £3000 in cash on the dresser as he left.

Luke crosses the road and knocked on Marion's door, hoping to renew there old friendship yet again, but received no answer, as she was obviously out.

Next, he drove into Worcester to see Trudy, the big car attracting much attention as he drew up outside her house in Canterbury road, Ronkswood.
Tracy came hurtling up the steps and flew into his outstretched arms.

" Dad. Dad. Oh God. It's great to see you again."

She kissed him full on the lips and hugged him tightly.

" Oh God. Come on in. Mum's out, but won't be too long."
" How's you Tracy?"
" Oh. I'm fine."
" You certainly looks it, baby."

They walked down the path arm in arm and into the kitchen. The young man sitting at the table simply stared, and Luke grinned at him, knowing instantly what was going through his insecure mind.

Luke squeezed Tracy tightly and kissed her on the cheek.

" A friend of yours, babe?"

She giggled.

" Yes. Meet Dave."
" Hi Dave."
" Hello."

The sullen voice was flat and low.

" Dave, this is Lou."

Dave didn't answer and Luke sat opposite him with Tracy perched upon his knee, her arm around his neck.

" Oh, Lou. It's been ages since I've seen you."
" Yeh. Sorry, babe. Things turn up, and off I goes."
" Well. You're here now. How long are you staying?"
" Long enough for a cup of coffee."

" Oh. Sorry. I was so chuffed to see you. I'll make you one now."

She slipped away and Luke turned to Dave.
The young man's eyes were blazing and his jaw set as he spoke.

" How long you known Tracy for?"
" Hell. Can't remember, Davy, boy. Years and years. And you, how long you known her for?"
" Just over 18 months."
" Like her, does you?"
" pardon?"
" I said. Does you like her?"
" Well. Yes. Course I do."
" That's okay then. I only wants to know. How old is you?"
" Twenty Three."
" You workin?"
" Yeh, when I can get it. I'm a mechanic."
" A good one?"
" Yeh. I think so, anyway."
" Not a lot of work around here though, is there?"
" Sod all really. I have to make up doing free-lance stuff."
" Get your own garage."
" Oh yeh. What with, bloody marbles."

Tracy brought the coffees over and sat back down on Luke's knee.

He squeezed her around the waist gently.

" This your young man then, is it, babe?"

" Well. Yes. He is really. Do you like him?"

" Yeh. seems okay."

" Not up to your own hell raising standards though?"

" Just as well for you, probably, babe."

" Tracy. Are we still going out tonight?"

" Yes. Of course we are, Dave. Why?"

" Well. I just wondered. You seem to be, well, occupied, that's all."

Luke laughed.

" I'll tell you somethin, boy. If I'd have been you and this happened to me, I'd have just about broke you in half by now."

Dave half rose, his fists clenched and Tracy hastily pushed him back into his seat.

" Leave him, Dave. He'll kill you.

" I can fight my own battles, thanks."

Luke grinned.

" I admire your bottle, mate, but leave it out, will you?"

" What. When you two are messin about and you're tryin to steal my girl."

" Listen. Why would I want to do that?"

" You tell me. But you seem to be doing it."

" Arsehole."

" Dad. Please."

Dave looked from one to the other, puzzlement in his troubled eyes.

" Dad? Did you say, Dad?"

Dave's eyes widened even more, and his jaw dropped.

" Dad? You're her Dad?"

" Ha. Yeh. Hey, Tracy. Why'd you have to let that slip. I was just startin to enjoy meself then?"

" Oh. Sorry, Lou."

She buried her head into Luke's shoulder as she collapsed into uncontrollable laughter.

Dave shook his head nervously.

" Hell. I'm sorry, Lou. Mr Brown."

" Lou will do, mate. No sweat. Just my little joke. My sick sense of humour."

" Oh. That's okay. Tracy's always on about you. I should have guessed. Anyway, I've got to fly now, we've a rush job on this afternoon."

When Tracy returned from seeing Dave off, she plonked herself down on Luke's lap once more and hugged him tightly to her.

" Oh. It really is great to see you again. It really is."
" Same here, Tracy, babe."

Luke kissed her forehead and she clung to him even more tightly.

" It's hard to think of you as my Dad, you know."
" That much of a disappointment, am I?"
" No. Silly. No one believes that you're old enough. You're more of a friend than a parent."
" Wot about Trudy?"
" Oh. She's definitely my Mum. Acts like one, too."
" I bet she'll be pleased to hear that. Where's Mary these days?"
" Oh. She's around. She'll be up soon, if you want to see her?"
" Yeh. Be nice."

" Yes. I imagine it will. Oh, by the way. Did you know that she had a baby?"

Luke stared hard at Tracey as she grinmned back at him.

" Wot?"
" Yes. That's what we all said. She won't tell anyone who the Father is, though."
" Jeez."
" Yes. He's, what, oh, about four now."
" He?"
" Yes. It's a boy. Seth, she called him. He's so lovely. Why?"
" Oh. Nothin."
" Dad. What are you thinking?"
" Nothin, babe."
" No. I bet. The same as me, I expect?"
" Wot's that?"
" That it's yours."

Luke almost fell off the chair upon hearing this and Tracy's grin widened by several inches

" Oh. Come on Dad. He looks exactly like I did at that age and, Mum and Mary aren't exactly the close friends that they once were."
" Oh shit."

" Don't worry. Mum's a bit peeved, but she'll survive. Like she said, she should have expected it off you."

Her laughing voice took away the sting from her words and she rose.

" Here's Mary and Seth now by the sound of it.

Mary stopped dead in the doorway, her eyes wide and cheeks flushed.
Luke grinned and opened his arms wide.

" Mary, babe."

She was in his arms instantly and they kissed long and hard, their bodies pressed tightly together. At last, they broke and Luke kissed the tip of her nose.

" Baby. I've only just found out about little Seth."
" Oh, Lou. I didn't really want you to know."
" Why not. He's mine, ain't he?"
" Of course he is."
" Well then. A boy at last, Mary. My only Son."
" Honestly?"
" Yeh, honest."
" Oh, Lou. And it had to be me."
" Yeh, great, ain't it?"

Luke played with his small Son for a while then, reluctantly, he rose to leave, looking at Mary as she smiled at him.

" How's you fixed for dosh, Mary?"
" Well. Okay. Why?"
" Yeh? Don't believe you."

Luke took out his cheque book and began writing.

" You got a bank account, babe, in your own name?"
" Yes."

After finishing, Luke handed her the cheque and winked at her.

" That's for both of you. Okay?"
" God. Lou. I can't take this off you."
" You just did. And you'll take more before I've finished."
" But it's for £10,000.?"
" So? It's only money, babe. Mary. I want to look after you and Seth properly, okay?"

Luke left as quickly as he could after kissing all three of them and promising to keep in touch.

Chapter 3

The old gym was closed and deserted now, and Luke parked in the top car park once again, sitting in the car and looking through the local Worcester newspaper that he had bought.

A tap at the window made him look up top see the top half of Tom grinning in at him.

Luke opened the window and thrust his hand out, gripping Tom's firmly.

" Hey, mate. How's it goin?"

" Lou. Fuckin hell, man. I thought you was dead. Wot are you doin back here?"

" Come back to fuckin well haunt you, you tosser."

" Yeh. I thought it was your mush I could see. A fuckin Jag now. Whoo. Times must be good, yeh?"

" So. So. You know. Anyway, how's your life hangin?"

" Well. I'm still here. Just. Quack says I have to give up fags and booze. I asks you, wot the fuck else is there besides them?"

" Shaggin."

" Oh yeh. Last leg over I had was when I fell off me pissin bike. And that was in 86."

" T'aint that bad, is it, mate?"

" Naw. Not really. You knows me, always lookin on the bright side. Anyway. You stayin round here now?"

" Naw. Doubt it. I'm stayin at Derr's and Mo's for a few days."

" Fuckin hell. You shafted Mo yet, finally?"

" Piss off."

" Yeh. I bet you would, if you ain't already. Anyway, look, man. I has to split as I've got to go to Hereford Hospital for a check up on me legs, that I ain't got. You know. I still can't get used to this fuckin wheelchair. I'll see you around, Lou."

" Sure. Take care, mate."

It was 3.20pm when Luke arrived back at Derrick's and after grabbing a cup of coffee and a kiss off Mo, he settled down to look at the Bromyard local paper again, and chat to her until tea time.

Mo was going to her neighbours to babysit that evening and Derrick wasn't due back until the following day at least, though Mo was vague as his real whereabouts, so Luke did not press her.

Apparently, Debbie was off out somewhere, as she bustled around to and fro. She had lost her friendliness of the day before and totally ignored Luke now, passing him silently as he went through to the front room.

Mo grinned at him as she passed on her way out and bent to kiss Luke lightly on his lips.

" Thought I'd return the compliment, Lou. Yummy."

Then she was gone, and Luke wondered what to do that evening.

Luke decided to go down town and left at around 7.30pm, just to see what was about these days.

His first stop was the Bay Horse but, after some fifteen minutes, he left, as it had changed so much over the years, even the beer tasted different now, he mused.

His next stop was The Falcon, and he stood at the bar sipping his pint and gazing around.
This place, too, had changed, and he saw the new landlady eying him coolly. He winked over at her and she turned away without a reaction and Luke grinned to himself at the stoney expression on her face.

The juke box was booming and Luke saw that it was mostly teenagers in the bar these days, as it had been in his day, really.

Through the open archway into the middle bar, Luke caught sight of an old school acquaintance and crossed through to speak to him and his wife.

Their two daughters sat with them and, as he introduced himself, saw their interest quicken. He soon tired of the same old lines from them, work, money, cars, mowing the lawn, and saving for holidays. God, he was so piss-bored with these people. Why had they stopped living? They merely existed now, it seemed. Was this what married life and middle age did to you, make you lose all interest in life in general?

Luke soon returned to the bar, finding that it was filling up rapidly. By 8.30pm the bar was packed and alive with chatter and music and Luke sat back against the bar remembering how it used to be back in the 60's when he was a regular in there and working behind this very bar.

The landlady stopped to grab some bottles and looked at Luke again.

" Do you always smile to yourself?"
" Yeh. Depends wot I'm thinkin of, mind."
" I see."
" Thought you was goin to turf me out earlier, you was lookin at me a bit hard?"
" Hmm. Just checking."
" Yeh? Hey, girl. I used to work in here."
" Oh yes. Did you?"
" Yeh. Years ago. Before you was born."
" Oh,. I see. One of those, are you. Anything for a free drink."
. Naw. Not quite. You ain't local, is you, girl?"
" No. I'm from Lichfield. I've been here about three years now."
" Yeh? Old Percy used to be here when I was here. Oh. I'm Lou, by the way."

" And I'm Sally."

" Right. Hi there Sall. Used to know one, once."

" Oh yes. I'm sure that you did. When was it that you worked here?"

" Oh. About twenty odd years ago now."

" Oh yes. Seriously."

" Yeh. Honest, babe."

Her brow went into a quick frown as she studied him, then she shrugged.

" Okay. If you say so, Now, I must get on."

Luke had the distinct impression that Sally didn't believe him and grinned to himself, perhaps he did, indeed look too young, as all of his friends had said?

He hoisted himself off the stool and walked through to the telephone booth in the front bar, winking at his friends two Daughters as he passed, making them giggle loudly, their parents having left.

After dialling, Luke found that the number he required was no longer available and came out of the booth deep in thought.

" Lou. It is you, ain't it?"

" Hells bells. Tommy Roberts. Wot you doin in the front bar?"

" Ha. I'm a rich farmer now. Hell. I thought it was your Son for a minute. You ain't changed a bit, you know that. Wot's it been, twenty, twenty two years?"

" Yeh, somethin like that."

" Wot's the secret? Still shaggin yourself stupid, I expect. Keeps you young though, I'll give you that."

" Yeh."

Luke winked at Sally as she breezed through the bar and Tommy grinned.

" You've met her, I take it?"

" Oh yeh. We've met."

" Watch her, she's hell on wheels, mate."

" Yeh? She's a bit young for me, ain't she?"

Sally pretended not to hear this, though she obviously did, and Luke slapped Tommy on the back.

" Want a drink, Tom?"

" It's okay, Lou. I'm off in a minute. Another time?"

" Yeh."

Luke returned to the back bar and found the two giggling girls there, gazing at him with wide eyes as he sat back on his stool.

He winked at them and grinned as they stood next to him at the bar.

" You two want a drink?"

" Oh, yeh. Thanks, Lou."

" Wot's your name's , then?"

" I'm Ruth. That's Manda."

" Hi both. Wot do you want to drink then?"

" Shandy, if you can get it. Orange juice if you can't."

" I'll get it. Go and park your arses over there."

Luke brought the drinks over to them, grinning.

" See. Easy when you knows how. You shouldn't drink anyway at your age."

" You did."

" Oh yeh. Been hearin tales, has you?"

" And how."

" Ha. Well. Enjoy yourselves, ladies and don't do nothin I'd do."

Luke crossed to the bar, regained his stool and sat with his back to the bar, quietly smoking and listening to the music as it boomed out continuously.

The place was absolutely jam-packed now and the two barmaids were kept flat out as they tried to clear the back-log of queuing customers who stood at the bar.

They eyed Luke occasionally, but neither spoke as they rushed back and forth across the bar.

Sally poked her head through from the front as Luke held up his empty glass and, as one of the girls came forward, Sally swept past and took his glass.

" I owe you an apology, Lou Brown."
" Oh. Last names too, now, is it. Wot's yours?"
" Appleton."
" Miss?"
" We haven't progressed that far yet, Lou."
" Okay. Sorry, babe."
" Okay. This one's on the house. I've been hearing quite a lot about you from certain members of the front bar."
" Yeh? I was afraid of that. You can't have heard it all, else you'd ban me."
" I think I have. I'm not sure that I believe it all, mind. Anyway. I must fly."

Luke sipped his pint thoughtfully and grinned at the two barmaids, making them smile in return.

He picked up his ears as an old Jim Diamond song came on, ' I Should Have Known Better' and joined in, as did most of the customers, when the ' Iy, Yi, Yi, Yi, Yi's' came on in the song.

Lighting up a smoke, Luke turned and scanned the room. Ruth and Manda were sat amongst their friends and waved at him as they caught his eye. He had obviously been the topic of discussion, for all ten of them turned to study him quickly before turning away again.

Luke's gaze travelled on and he decided that there were far more women in the bar than men. Quite the opposite from his day.

The dartboard was in full use and Luke watched as the game progressed, very slowly at times.

One youth was shouting loudly, eager to play anyone for a fiver.

Luke crossed and plucked the darts from his fingers.

" Let's see your money, mate."
" Eh?"
" Show us your fiver, then I'll play you."
" Oh yeh. here."

He held it up and Luke took it and, together with his own, handed them to one of the girls who was standing watching them.

" Here, baby. Hold this and give it to the winner. Okay?"
" Yeh. Okay."

Luke turned to the youh.

" Can I have a practise throw. I'm a bit rusty?"
" Sure."

Luke threw loosely at the board, hitting it here and there and turned, grinning, to the lad.

" Okay. nearest the bull for off?"
" Yeh."

The other threw and scored a 25, to loud applause from his friends.

Luke simply stood and shot, scoring a dead-centre, bull.

Luke winked at the girls and shot his three darts, scoring a bull away and two treble twenties.

" `170 away, leaves 131. Right?"
" Yeh."

The other didn't get away and Luke's next shots wer deadly accurate.

Treble 19. Double 18 and a double 9 for out.

" That do you, pal?"

His opponent didn't answer.

" Fancy another. Double or quits?"
" Huh. No thanks."

Luke turned and took the £10 from the grinning girl.

" Thanks, baby. Come on. I'll buy you lot a drink."

When they were all refilled, Luke left them alone and sat at the bar again smoking and listening to the music.

A fresh wave of customers arrived, bursting through the door and jamming the bar even more.

It was some 15 minutes later that he turned in response to a dig in his ribs.

It was Ruth, grinning at his side.

" We're off now, Lou. Thanks for the drink."
" Okay, babe. Where you lot off?"
" Up the dance."
" Where at?"
" Saltmarshe."
" Jeez. They still have them there?"
" Yeh. Why don't you come?"
" Yeh. I might do, later."
" I'll buy you a drink if you do. Byee."
" Yeh, catch you again, babe."

They all waved at him, and the place was 10 bodies less, but still crowded to bursting point.

Coming back to his stool from the toilet, Luke saw Debbie leaning against the juke box, a bored expression across her face. She was with the last group that had arrived and they now sprawled themselves out along the benches and tables over by the window.

She didn't respond to Luke's smile as their eyes met, and he turned away.

Sally was rummaging on some of the shelves.

" Damn. We'll have to get the other crates up now."

Luke smiled.

" I'll get them for you, Sal."

Sally looked at him thankfully.

" Oh, Lou. Will you?"
" Yeh. No sweat."
" They're down the cellar. Here, I'll show you."
" I knows me way round there, baby."
" Oh yes. Two cases of Light Browns and a case of Pony, please, Sir."

Luke soon had them up and grinned at Tommy, who was still stationed at the front bar.

" Hey, Lou. You back serving behind the bar, then?"

" Oh yeh."

" God help us all. Watch your change, folks."

Luke laughed as he passed under the flap into the back bar once more, finding that someone else had claimed his stool.

He collected several of the empty glasses from the tables, depositing them on the bar.

Sally grabbed his empty glass and refilled it.

" On me, okay."

" Anytime, babe."

" pardon?"

" A joke."

Then she was gone, rushing back into the front bar and its usual mayhem.

Luke crossed to the juke box and scanned the record titles, watched by the silent Debbie who stood at his elbow.

Without speaking to her, Luke made his selections and returned to the crowded bar counter. He moved to the window, his glass in his hand and listened as Jim Diamond started up, followed by Chicago, then Phil Collins ' Against All Odds'. Still standing there, gazing at nothing in particular, Luke listened to the other tunes as they played. Then the box fell silent momentarily, starting up once more with Jim Diamond again.

Luke saw Debbie still selecting hers and lit up a smoke as he repossessed his, now empty, stool.

Sally appeared once more, her cheeks flushed and Luke gazed at her.

She stood some 5ft 6ins tall with short, curly, light brown hair, with eyes the same colour.

Luke guessed that she was in her early 30's.

Her deep blue dress suited her perfectly and Luke saw her long, slim, legs as she re-crossed the bar.

" Inspection over, is it. How did I do?"

Sally stood, hefting a crate aside so as to get to the bottles on the shelf behind.

" Yeh. You did okay."
" Oh. Good. Bit young for you though, aren't I?"

She was gone before he could reply and Luke grinned to himself.

" Lou. You tit suckin arsehole. How is you, mate?"

Luke turned and saw Ferret standing in the doorway.

" Fuckin hell. You still pissed?"
" Yeh. Wot else is there to do in this pox hole?"

" Want a drink?"

" Naw. Can't come in, can I? Sort of banned, ain't I."

" I'll catch you again then, mate."

" Yeh. You do that, Lou. We can catch up on the last few years."

Luke returned to his drink as ' I Should Have Known Better' boomed out yet again and Luke turned to see Debbie at the juke box once more. A loud cheer went up as she flopped into a seat, slightly the worse for wear, Luke thought. A round was bought for all of her group and the noise increased by several decibels.

Luke crossed to the juke box and put on Steve Wonder's ' I Just Called To Say I love You', ignoring Debbie as he turned away, and leaned against the juke box, humming quietly to the song as he smoked.

" Scuse me."

One of Debbie's group squeezed past him and fed more money into the box. She laughed and called to Debbie.

" I suppose you want that Jim Diamond on again? I never knew you liked it. You never played it before?"

Debbie didn't reply and Luke returned to the bar, reflecting that most of the records seemed to be ballad's on the juke box these days.

Then Frankie Goes To Hollywood came on and ' The Power Of Love' boomed out and filled the bar, Luke joining in.

Sally grinned as she pused before him.

" Quite a singer, too."
" Keeps my mind from wanderin."
" I won't ask what to, or from."

Luke passed his empty glass to one of the barmaids and she grinned.

" Don't remember me, do you, Lou?"
" Nope. Not yet, I don't."

She blushed and placed his full pint before him.

" On the house, so the boss says. I'm Mike Thomson's Daughter."
" Jeez. Not little Mike. Who's you, then, baby?"
" Judy."
" Hi, Judy. Okay, ain''t you?"
" Am I?"
" Oh yeh."

She moved away, giggling, and Luke sipped at his fresh drink.

Debbie's group finally made a move and she rose slowly to her feet. Luke watched her as she passed him.

" Have a good time, Debs."

She carried on, then came slowly back, peering at him.

" I'm going to the dance."
" Well. At least you're speakin to me again."
" I always was. I thought you were ignoring me."
" Hardly, babe. How the fuck could anyone ignore you."
" Oh."
" I likes your choice in records, girl."

Debbie blushed.

" I have to go or I'll miss my lift."
" I'll take you up there, if you like."

She hesitated, then shook her head, gazing intently at him.

" I don't think that you better had, thanks all the same, Lou."

" No sweat, baby."

The door reopened.

" You comin, or not, Deb?"

" Yes."

Luke turned away and sipped his drink once more as Debbie followed her friend out. He rose and collected more empty glasses, returning them, to the bar.

He grinned at Sally.

" Here. Don't say I don't do nothin for you."

" Thanks, Lou."

" Anytime, baby."

" Tha's the second time that you've said that to me."

" Is that all, Sal?"

Sally was gone once more and Luke caught Judy's eye and winked, starting her off into giggles again.

Jim Diamond came on once more and Luke turned.

There stood Debbie with her back to him as she faced the juke box. Her knuckles were white as she gripped the sides of the machine tightly.

Ambling over to her, Luke leaned against the wall next to Debbie.

" Like this record, don't you? Like I said, you've a good taste in music. Want a drink, babe?"
" I. I don't think so."
" Sure? Shan't ask again."
" Oh. Okay. A Pony, please."

Bringing it back to her, Luke perched on the edge of the wooden beam that stuck out of the wall near the fireplace and rested his feet on the side of the throbbing juke box.

" Smoke?"
" No thanks."

Luke flicked his lighter closed and drew a deep lungful of smoke in.

" I'll run you up the dance in a minute."
" Oh, yes. Thanks."
" Missed the other lift, did you?"
" Oh. Yes. Yes, I did."
" Bit crowded, I expect?"
" Yes. Something like that."

They left soon afterwards and Luke held the passengerdoor open for Debbie, the white Jaguar gleaming brightly in the sodium lights as Luke eased the car out into Pump Street, turning right to travel down Broad Street.

" Straight to the dance, or do you want to stop off anywhere else first, babe?"
" I don't mind, Lou, thanks."

Luke pressed in a tape and the machine started playing a Chicago tape and Debbie leaned back against the seat with her eyes closed.

" You okay, Debs?"
" What? Yes. Oh, yes thanks."

She had shot bolt upright as Luke had spoken and now settled back to her former position, this time with her eyes wide open and gazing at some unknown part of the cars roof.

Luke drew into the Saltmarsh Village Hall car park, selecting a spot near the roadside.

Lights blazed out of the windows as people walked, ran, stood together or simply sat on the wooden railings outside the hall.

Things hadn't changed since Luke's youth when he came here, only the cars were different, he thought, also noticing the complete lack of motorcycles present.

" Well. We're here, baby."
" Thanks."

Luke lit up another cigarette and lay back to listen to the music once more.

" Are you going in?"
" Naw. Doubt it, babe.. Unless you wants me too, that is?"

Debbie shrugged.

" It's up to you, isn't it?"
" Do you want me to?"
" I don't mind. I told you."
" Who's runnin it?"
" Young farmers."
" Yeh? Magic. Think I'll stroll in after all."

At the door, Luke paid for them both, watching as Debbie continued on through to the hall without waiting for him.

The doorman eyed Luke carefully.

" You don't remember me, do you?"

" Nope."

" I'm one of those who you gave a hiding too, way back."

" Yeh? You seems okay now."

" Oh yeh. My old man didn't half give me a hiding afterwards though.

He broke into a grin and Luke took the outstretched hand.

" How are you then, Lou?"

" Okay, pal. Nigel, ain't it?"

" Yeh."

" How is your old man, these days?"

" Oh. He's okay. Works too bloody hard but, apart from that, he's well. You're a stranger round here these days, ain't you?"

" Yeh. I comes and goes."

" There's a few you might recognize inside, especially one, serving behind the buffet bar."

Luke took his leave and wandered through the hall. Debbie had joined her friends by now and was in the centre of their group. Their eyes turned towards him as Luke entered and he grinned over at them.

Just as in his day, the floor still vibrated to the loud music and Luke felt the bass notes thumping out of the huge speakers, his teeth almost rattling as he passed in front of them.

The buffet bar was located in the long back room and, already, it was doing a brisk trade.

Luke aimed himself through the crowd at the bar but less than halfway through felt a tug at his sleeve and a hand upon his arm.

" Lou. God. It is you."

Luke gazed back at the women who had stopped him and smiled.

" Rachel. Jeez. You've shot up, baby, ain't you?"

Luke grabbed her and hugged Rachel tightly to him, crushing his lips against hers.

" Lou. Please. Not here."
" Sorry."
" Yes. Well."

Rachel pushed a hand through her hair and smoothed down her dress as she stepped away from him.

" I'm a married woman now."
" Shit. Is your old man here?"

" Yes. He's on the door."

" Wot, Nigel?"

" Yes."

Luke laughed loudly and explained to the mystified Rachel, who smiled back.

" Yes. That's the sort of thing he would do. Nigel's okay, really."

" Not bad for a farmer?"

" Lou. You used to like farms."

" I still does. How's your Mum?"

" Oh. She's okay, thanks. It's funny, you know, talking of her. Remember that dance when your little French friend was there?"

" Yeh. Vaguely."

" Well. Mum's never mentioned you since then. Before that, she was always on to me about you."

" Perhaps she realised that I was harmless?"

" Or, perhaps she realised something else, too?"

" Meanin?"

" Nothing."

" She ain't here?"

" God no. She's 57 now."

" Jeez."

" Quite."

" Ha. Not you as well, babe, please."

" Go and see her, Lou, if you like. She alone there, it isn't far and she'd love to see you, after all this time."

" Wot about you?"

" I'll be here when you get back. We can talk then, if you want?"

" Oh yeh, believe it, I does, not only talkin, neither."

Grinning at Rachel's expression, Luke winked at Nigel as he passed and drove off in the car.

The farm track was as he remembered it and Luke gently re-closed the old road gate.

The house showed just one light at the rear and Luke knocked gently at the kitchen door, setting several dogs of barking loudly from within.

A female voice at once silenced them and Luke instantly recognized Elizabeth's voice as she came to the door.

" Who's there?"

" Tis I, Lisbeth."

" Who is it?"

" An old friend, baby."

The silence was absolute, then the door opened fractionally.

" Lou."

Elizabeth threw the door wide as she unhooked the chain and stood before him, her mouth open.

Meeting her halfway, they embraced warmly. She had aged, Luke could see that. But if he didn't know better, he would have said that Elizabeth was no more than 45.

Luke tilted her head up to his as he kicked the door shut with one foot.

" You alone?"
" Yes. Why?"

`Luke bent to her and kissed her parted lips. At first she tried to pull away but as Luke pressed on, Elizabeth wrapped her arms around his neck and began to respond to his probing tongue, clingint to him tightly.

" God. It's years since I've been kissed like that, Lou."

Luke repeated it and she responded instantly, moulding her body to Luke's as he pressed himself tightly to her.

Without speaking, Luke picked her up and carried her forward.

" Lou. What are you doing?"

Luke mounted the stairs .

" Where's your bedroom, babe?"
" Oh. God. First one on the left."

Luke entered the room and set Elizabeth gently down on her bed. Sitting beside her, Luke leant over and kissed her parted lips.

" Lou."
" Don't say nothin, babe. Just remember."

Luke stood up and quickly closed the door, returning to the bedside as he undressed in the darkness.

Kneeling over her on the bed, Luke began to undress Elizabeth and, as she touched Luke's naked body, gasped and, with a little cry, began to eagerly help Luke.

Luke began to kiss and caress her naked body and, although Elizabeth was slow to respond at first, she soon forgot her inhibitions and became the Elizabeth of old that Luke remembered from all of those years ago.

Elizabeth soon bought all of her experience to bear and they enjoyed a heady love-making session that left them both gasping with pleasure.

As they caressed and stroked each other, Elizabeth slid over Luke and eased herself down on his solid growth, leading them, once more, on another wild adventure of passion.

On they pumped, reaching climax after climax and their sweating bodies worked together on the crumpled sheets as Elizabeth brought Luke on to, yet another, frantic climax as he lay deep within her welcoming body.

When they were finally lying, still, together, Elizabeth moaned as she kissed Luke's ear.

" Oh, Lou. I feel so young again. This has brought it all back me to, after all these years."

She started to sob and Luke comforted her, stroking her soft hair.

" Hey, c'mon, babe. Don't be sad."
" Oh. I'm not. I'm so happy, Lou."
" Baby, I still remembers that first night with you."
" So do I, Lou, my angel. It was sheer heaven. I was so worried that you would boast about it to your friends."
" Hey. No way, Elizabeth. I had more respect for you than that. Wot do you take me for, an idiot?"
" Quite."

They both fell together laughing, and Luke kissed her lovely body, running his tongue down past her stomach and making Elizabeth arch up beneath him in pleasure.

" Oh Lou. Will you come again?"

" Wot. Tonight?"

" Lou. You know very well what I mean. Will you come and see me again, another day?"

" Yeh. Course I will, if you wants me to, girl?"

" You know that I do. And, as for coming again tonight. Let me see what I can do to assist you there."

Elizabeth pulled Luke down to her and he felt himself sliding easily into her receptive body once more. They made a slow meal of their remaining passions until Luke lay deep within her, spent at last.

Luke flicked on the light and stood gazing down at Elizabeth's flushed face and supple body.

" You don't really look no older than me, honestly, babe."

" It's only thanks to you, then, Lou, my love."

Her eyes took in Luke's body and she leant over to kiss his drooping growth before taking it into her mouth.

It instantly rose up again and she chuckled wickedly as her lips worked him.

" Here we go again, Lou."

One last time Luke met with her, Elisabeth on top again, and it was a beautiful ending to their brief passionate session of love.

" Oh, Lou. I'm going to have a nice shower to cool off. Are you coming?"
" Wot. Again?"
" Lou. Please."

In the shower, they soaped each other and kissed amongst the bubbles and Luke lifted Elizabeth off her feet as he entered her against the wall, both laughing with the excitement of it all between them.

Dried at last, they dressed and descended to the kitchen, where they sat opposite each other as they drank their coffee.

" Rachel will be glad to see you again."
" I've seen her already. At the dance."
" Oh. I see."
" She suggested that I call and see you."
" Oh. Did she now? Lou. Did you ever make love to her?"
" Wot?"

" Oh. Come on, Lou. Don't go all vague. It doesn't matter after all this time."

" Wot did she tell you?"

" Nothing. Of course."

" There you goes then."

" Lou."

" Okay. Jeez. Look, we, sort of, got it together occasionally."

" Sort of?"

" Yeh, well, yeh. Okay."

" Haha. I always thought that you did, somehow."

" She was a nice girl."

" She still is."

" Yeh. So I noticed."

" Lou. She's happily married, too."

" Okay. Okay. I gets the hint."

They kissed for long minutes at the door and Luke left Elizabeth feeling ten years younger.

Luke arrived back at the dance, finding that a big argument was taking place at the door.

The two door keepers were surrounded by eight jeering, leather-jacketed youths, who were obviously the worse for drink.

" And I say, you fuckin carrot crunchers, that we are goin in."

" I'm sorry, but you've been told before…"

" Listen you cunt…"

Luke moved forward and spun the mouth around to face him.

" You deaf, you mother fucker?"

" Wot? Fuck you, piss head."

Luke head butted him twice in rapid succession and, as he slid to the floor screaming, kneed him hard between the legs.

He whirled around and chopped another to the throat as he kicked another just under the left kneecap and, as he also fell, delivered a crushing fist to the side of his head.

Luke grabbed two more and, bringing them together, smacked their heads together with sickening force.

The rest simply backed away and stood, wide eyed and riveted with fear, staring as Luke approached.

" Right. Get these piles of shit out of here, now. And, if I hear you arseholes causin any more trouble, I'll fuckin well destroy you all. Okay?"

They nodded and started to help their fallen friends to their feet as Luke turned away.

He winked at Nigel.

" Piss easy, or wot?"
" Christ, Lou. We must have been bloody mad to cross you in the old days?"
" Naw. It was all a bit of fun, mate."

Luke stared at the assembled crowd and a murmur ran through them as they started to disperse, seeing that the action was over for the night. Luke pushed his way through them back into the dance hall, sighing deeply as he went.

As he felt a slight touch on his arm, Luke whirled around, ready for action again.

" Lou. Are you okay?"
" Rachel. Yeh. No sweat, babe."

Nigel appeared and grinned.

" God. Rachel. What a fighting machine. Thanks, Lou. You saved us a lot of trouble out there."
" Yeh. All part of the service, mate."

Nigel moved back towards the door and Rachel fastened her arm through Luke's.

" Come on, let me get you something to eat."

Luke saw many eyes upon him as they walked through the hall. A few of the youngsters were demonstrating some of Luke's moves on their friends, but when they felt his eyes on them, simply grinned sheepishly and moved away.

Rachel plied him with sandwiches and coffee and generally fussed around him in a concerned manner.
At last she was satisfied as she gazed into his eyes.

" Well. At least the battle lights have gone out of your eyes now. You really are a fighting machine when you get going, aren't you?"
" Well. No use stopping to talk, is it?"
" So. How was Mother?"
" Oh. Good as ever."
" Lou."
" Sorry. We had a long chat and a cup of coffee. She's okay, ain't she?"
" How?"
" Well. I mean, bright and cheerful."
" It must have been you that was the tonic then?"
" Naw. She don't look her age, though."

" No wrinkles?"

" None that I could see."

" That, dear, Lou. Depends upon where you looked."

" Oh yeh?"

" Yes."

" Jeez. It's hot in here, ain't it?"

" Lou. I am not going outside with you. I'm a married woman, now."

" So? Wot you think I wants to do?"

" Lou. Don't say another word."

" Well. Jeez."

" Now. Now."

" Or later."

" Lou. Behave, please."

" Arsehole. Get out through a window if you don't want your old man to know."

" Lou. Stop it. I am not going outside with you, and that's that."

" Okay. I'll catch you later then, misery."

" Huh. Oh, hang on. I'll nip out of the back door and meet you by the gate at the side of the car park."

Luke sat in the XJS and waited for Rachel to appear. Seeing her, he drove slowly forward and opened the passenger door for her.

" Lou. Is this your car?"

" Yeh."
" Good God."

She got in and slammed the door as Luke quickly accelerated away down the road.

" Where are we going, Lou?"
" Dunno., Anywhere, long as it's quiet."
" Lou."
" Just for a talk. Okay?"

Further down the road Luke gunned the big motor and they were soon parked up beneath the dark bulk of Warren Wood.
Luke grinned over at her.

" One of our old spots."
" I don't wish to know, thank you."
" Okay. Anyway. How's you these days, baby?"
" I'm okay, thanks, Lou. Things seem to be going well."
" Any family?"
" Yes. We've four children, two girls and two boys. And you?"
" Yeh."
" Yes, what?"
" Yeh. Just, yeh."

Luke restarted the Chicago tape and leaned over towards Rachel.

" Now. Can I finish my greetin?"
" Lou. Do you really think you ought to?"
" Fuckin hell, girl."

His lips met Rachel's as they tasted each other for several seconds before locking their lips tightly together in a strong, firm, embrace.

Luke reclined her seat before doing the same to his own and ran his hands expertly over her body.

" Lou."
" Shh, baby. Just kiss me."

Her lips met Luke's and their heads twisted as their embrace intensified, Rachel's lips seeking his hungrily now as her old passion for him became aroused.

Luke flicked his tongue over her ear and Rachel pulled away, stopping Luke's wandering hands with hers.

" Lou. No. This isn't right."

Luke kissed her tenderly once more and she sighed deeply, throwing her arms around his neck tightly as she probed him with her tongue.

Luke's fingers moved over her, feather light and gentle, tracing a line down her leg and back up beneath her dress.

Rachel's legs automatically parted for him as Luke reached her knickers and she sighed deeply once more as her own hands sought him.

The beauty of the Jaguar was that it was big enough to move around in without difficulty, and they were soon enjoying, to the full, each other's bodies.

Rachel's climaxes were just as wild as they used to be, and she really rocked the car in her passion, crying out loudly as her mind blew in a climaxing frenzy of vocal pleasure.

As Luke shot deep inside her, Rachel tightened her muscles and held on to him even more firmly.

" Oh. Lou. Lou. This is years away, isn't it, just like it used to be. Have I got better, do you think?"

" You always was the best, my angel."

" Oh, Lou. You are so lovely, my love."

They made love once more before rearranging themselves as Luke drove back to the dancehall before anyone missed Rachel.

After one last, long, clinging, kiss, she was gone and Luke re entered the hall by the front door after having a leisurly smoke in the car as he mulled over the evening.

He glanced over casually as the stewards moved away from a group of youths who were noisily shouting.

Luke caught sight of a broken bottle and moved instantly, coming between the two groups as the youth moved forward.

" Wot's up, mate?"

The teenager stared at Luke through drink-fuddled eyes.

" These bastards are tryin to kick us out. Fuckin wankers."

" No need for the bottle though, is there?"

" Wot's it to you. You goin to be a hero and try to take it off me?"

" Naw. Look. You can get in all sorts of shit for this. You want to go down for GBH or worse."

" I don't give a fuckin shit."

" Wot. All because of a fuckin dance? You're willin to do bird, for that?"

" Fuck it, I say."

Luke moved forward, ignoring the bottle, and draped an arm about the swaying shoulders.

" Look. Give it to me and I'll buy you all a fuckin drink. You won't get kicked out. I promise you that."

" And if I fuckin-well don't?"

Luke bent his head closer to the other's ear.

" If you don't. You wake up in hospital, in a fuckin wheelchair. I ain't pissin you, neither."

The youth gazed at Luke, then at the crowd, then back at Luke. As he handed over the bottle an audible sigh went up through the dancefloor and Luke crossed to a waste bin, dropping it in before turning to the youths again.

" Okay. C'mon. Let's get you all that drink."

With the music back to full volume once more, Luke stood in the doorway near the stage, gazing idly around. Rachel smiled at him as she stopped.

" Busy night, Lou?"

" Yeh, just like old times, baby."

" Quite."

Luke continued to chat to Rachel for a while before moving out onto the dance floor again, sitting on the stage in front of the disco equipment.

The DJ bent towards him.

" Thanks for that, pal."

" No sweat."

" Fancy a request?"

" Yeh. Jim Diamond. ' I Should Have Known Better'"

" Okay. To anyone special?"

" Yeh. From Lou to Debbie."

" Consider it done, mate."

As the record finished the DJ's patter began, ending with.

" Now, a special request . Debbie, this is for you with lots of love from Lou."

Luke glanced up at him and shook his head at his wink.

As the music started, he lit up another smoke and watched as a group approached, Debbie in their midst.

She was definitely not sober now, and stood gazing down at the floor.

One of her friends grabbed Luke.

" Come on. You have to dance with her to this one, Lou."

They pushed them together, draping Debbie's arms over Luke's shoulders.

Luke ground out his smoke and wrapped his arms around her slim waist, joining the other smooching couples on the dancefloor.

Luke laid his head next to Debbie's and whispered gently into her ear.

" You okay, Deb?"
" Yes thanks."
" Hope you like the record?"
" Pig."
" Ha. Thanks for the compliment."

She bent her head and rested it on Luke's shoulder.

" Hmm. That's better. I feel a bit tizzy."
" Shame on you, baby."
" Oh. Belt up, will you, and dance."

They did, smoothly and easily and stayed together as the record ended.

The DJ struck up again.

" Well, folks. And, by popular demand, the next one is dedicated to Lou, from Debbie. With lots of, l o v e. It's Chicago, get smoochin."

As ' You're The Inspiration' started up, off they went again, and Debbie nuzzled into his ear, her warm breath stirring him.

Her quiet voice pleased Luke, and he turned his face to hers, their lips meeting in a tender, feather-light, first kiss. Debbie's words were lost in her throat and Luke pressed on, one hand behind her head now as he probed her warm, inviting, mouth.

Debbie became so still within his arms that Luke drew back to look at her. Her eyes were closed dreamily and she had a slight smile on her face.

" Hmm. Hmm."

They embraced once more, fully this time, stopping dancing as they became ever more engrossed in their kiss.

Luke overcame Debbie's inexperience at kissing by using his own skills and found her to be an eager pupil, her little tongue soon following his around.

When they broke at last a huge cheer went up from their friends and Debbie rested her head on Luke's shoulder, holding her arms high in the air.

Looking at the DJ, Debbie mouthed the words 'Chicago' then they were off once more in another dancing embrace.

Luke listened to Debbie as she quietly sang along and realized that, not only did she dance well, she was also a very good singer.

'Legs' came on next and two other girls moved in on Luke, but Debbie clung fiercely to him and he grinned at her face, staying silent.

Debbie turned to the DJ but was back with Luke within seconds.

" Well, folks. As the continuing saga of Lou and Debbie unfolds, here, with love from Debbie to Lou, is Stevie Wonder, telling us that he ' Just Called To say I Love You'."

Luke gazed deeply into Debbie's eyes as they started to dance once more, but she simply looked away and rested her head gently on Luke's shoulder again.

This time, her sweet voice came to Luke again, but this time he sang quietly along with her as their dancing slowed to a stop as they began to sing a duet.

At the end, all of the surrounding crowd clapped and cheered at their efforts and Debbie smiled.

" You've got a good voice, Lou."
" Not half as good as yours is, baby. Yours is brill."
" We ought to form a duet."

Luke grinned and kissed her hair lightly as the DJ sprang into life once more.

" Finally tonight for, yeh, you guessed it, Lou and Debbie, I give you Air Supply, telling us that they're ' All Out Of Love'."

Debbie smiled dreamily.

" I love this one, it's a great tune. How high can you go, Lou?"
" Not that fuckin high, babe. No way."

They sang in unison, quietly and together, the couples around them straining to catch their voices as the song progressed.

Luke suddenly realised that Debbie could really sing, her voice was so rich and sweet, ranging from a high, clear, soprano to a deep, throaty, and very sexy, croon.

The dance ended to more loud clapping for them and Luke kissed her once more as the hall began to empty.

" Comin home with me, babe?"
" I hope so."

She laughed and kissed Luke deeply, her eyes twinkling as she drew away, tottering unsteadily.

Her friends all waved at them as Luke drew away from the dance hall, noticing that someone had tied empty beer cans to the rear bumper.

After Luke had stopped to detach them, he climbed back into the XJS to find that Debbie had started the Air Supply tape off in the machine.

" Cmon. Babe. Let's hear you. I never knew that you could sing like that."

" I'm not that good."

" Yeh. Right."

" You're as good as me."

" Nowhere near, Debbie, babe."

" Let's say that we compliment each other, then, shall we?"

" Yeh. If you wants."

" Ate you musical, Lou?"

" A bit. I plays the drums and guitar a bit, and I fiddles around on the synth sometimes, too, but I ain't that good at any of it, only the drums, that is."

" Oh, good. You can help me work some tunes out. I do a lot of my own."

" So does I, well, when I gets the time to, that is."

" Great. We can work together at it, then."

Arriving back at Debbie's, they greeted Mo as Debbie rushed into the kitchen.

" Mum. You didn't say that Lou was musical?"

" I didn't know that he was, love. Are you drunk, miss?"

" No. Of course not, just a bit tipsy, wipsy, that's all. Mum. He's great. He can play, and sing and write. Come on, Lou. Let's go up to my bedroom."

Luke gazed at Mo and scratched his head.

" Me intentions is honorable, Mo, honest."

" Lou Brown. I wouldn't trust you as far as I could throw you."

" God. Mum. I can handle him, don't you worry. He's soft as a brush really."

Mo grinned over at Luke before replying.

"Debbie. It's gone 3.00am, don't you think that it's a bit late to start anything tonight?"

" Mum. I'll never rest. Oh. Wait, never mind. I'll fetch some of my stuff down here, if you're worried that we might get up to something in my bedroom."

Then she was gone, reappearing several minutes later with an arm crammed full of papers, a tape recorder, guitar and assorted cables.

Mo simply grinned and left to make them a drink.

She soon re entered with their coffee's and smiled at Luke.

" Good dance, lou?"

" Yeh. It was okay. Nice and quiet."

" Oh yeh? I've heard that one before, too."

" Mum. He put out seven men in leather jackets, and, took a broken bottle off another. A broken bottle, Mum. God, Lou is so brave."

" Ha. So, what's changed, eh, Lou?"

" Not a lot, has it, babe."

" Well. I'm off to bed. I'll leave you two musicians to it. And keep the noise down, too. Hey, Lou. This is good. I can boss you around now."

" Ha. Yeh. Don't worry. It's only borrowed. I'll just wait till you're bending down one day, then pay you back."

" Lou. Please."

" Sorry, Mo."

They both laughed as she left the room and Luke turned to Debbie.

She handed him a sheet of paper after sorting through the pile.

" What do you think of that?"

Luke read through the words, twice, digesting their plaintive meaning.

" Great, baby. I can't read music though."

" Oh. God, Lou. You duffer."

" I always uses a cassette to put my stuff on, humming, or strummin it, then I can alter it as I goes along if I has to."

" That's what I use, too. This is what the song goes like."

Debbie selected a cassette, put it in the recorder and pressed play.

She was playing her guitar with a backing dubbed on later and Luke listened as she sang the tune in a sad and tender voice.

As it ended, Debbie turned to Luke, her eyes bright and her smile wide.

" Come on. Tell me what you really think. The truth, mind."

" It was great. Honest. The minute I hears your voice, I'm lost. You could have a lousy tune and I wouldn't notice."

" Oh, Lou. You're no help, are you? I need an honest answer, Lou, not a load of fluff."

" Sorry, girl. I'll try a bit harder next time."
" Good. Okay, what can you do with this?"

Luke took the guitar from her and treated Debbie to a long bluesy intro.
She grinned.

" Oh. I say. Blues."
" Sorry."
" Belt up. I haven't got the feel for it myself. I can play it, but I think that you really have to, well, feel it, I suppose, to be able to play it as it's supposed to be played."
" Yeh. I think you're right, Deb."
" Well. At least we agree on something, that's a start."
" Can I read through the rest of your stuff, babe?"
" Sure."

Luke read through her words approvingly. One song in particular interested him, its words touching Luke deeply.

" This one's a bit sad, baby."
" Oh, wait. Come To Me. Is that the one?"
" Yeh."

" Hmm. I was trying to put over my own mood at the time. It takes me ages to write them, sometimes. How long does it take you?"

" Oh. Only about a few minutes usually."

" Honestly?"

" Yeh."

" Go on then."

" Now?"

" Why not? Do one about tonight at the dance."

" About us?"

" Yes."

" Okay. But play me this one first."

" Oh. Okay. But it isn't quite right yet."

The tape came on, and Luke listened intently to it, nodding afterwards.

" Yeh, its'okay, but a few words need changing around."

" Yes, Lou. I thought that, too."

" That last sentence in the second verse?"

" That's the one. Now, Lou. Get to it. Impress me."

Ten minutes later, Debbie was reading it through and smiled over at Luke as she pecked him on the cheek."

" This really is lovely, Lou. Honestly. You should be a poet, if you aren't already, that is?"

" Cheers, babe. Now you can write a tune for it."

" We, can. You mean. Oh. I'm so glad that I've found you, Lou."

" Feelin's mutual, Deb. Yeh. We'll make a good songwriting team."

She looked at Luke but didn't speak as she concentrated on tuning her guitar.

Luke made them some more coffee and, within twenty minutes, Debbie had a basic tune marked out, one that they were both happy with.

Debbie smiled broadly at him.

" Lou. This is great. I always get stuck for the words. So, if you do the lyrics, we can really turn out some good stuff, can't we?"

" Yeh. Sure. If you wants to, that is?"

" Oh yes. Let's at least give it a try, shall we?"

Luke lay back on the settee and lit up a smoke as Debbie continued to strum. Finally, she handed the guitar to Luke with a grin.

" Play me some blues, Lou. I love it, it's so expressive."

" Give us a kiss first, then."

Debbie brought her lips to Luke's and they clung together for several long minutes before she drew away, smiling warmly.

Luke flicked his dog-end expertly into the fire and picked up a plectrum and was soon well into a selection of tunes.

Debbie was smiling at him as she lay back next to him, her eyes never leaving his face. Leaning over, she lightly kissed his cheek again and lay back, sighing happily.

The next time that Luke looked at her he saw that Debbie had fallen fast asleep and, putting the instrument down, he covered her up with a coat from the hall. Then, turning the light off, Luke settled down on the floor beside her for the few remaining hours of the night.

Chapter 4

The following morning found them both stiff and grumpy. Mo only laughed at them as she passed their coffee.

" I told you to give it a rest last night, But, no, you wouldn't listen. Was it worth it?"

" Yes, Mum. Look. Lou wrote a beautiful song. I put the tune to it. It's lovely, read the words."

Mo's face softened as she read the words and she smiled as she handed the paper back to Debbie.

" It must have been some night, that's all I can say to you?"

Luke coughed as he remembered the words and even Debbie checked herself as she was about to reply, her cheeks reddening.

Luke grinned at Mo's enquiring gaze.

" Aw. C'mon, Mo. It was just somethin I wrote, to get the feelin, the mood. You know?"

" Oh yes. I understand, Lou. You don't have to explain it all to me. Remember, I know you. I was there."

Debbie shook her head, raising her eyes to the ceiling.

" God, Lou. What's the use? They're always jumping to the wrong conclusions. You just can't win with..... Oh God. I was going to say, with the older generation. But you're Mum's age, aren't you? I'm sorry. Though you look a lot younger then Mum does."

" Debbie. I suggest that you belt up, or you'll be doing a lot of housework today, and tomorrow, and the day after."

" Sorry, Mum. But, well. You just don't appreciate Lou's talent."

" Debbie, love. I do know where his talents lie, don't I Lou, dear?"

" Hey. C'mon, Mo. Fair crack of the whip here, yeh?"

" Haha. Okay. I accept that it's only a song and that your intentions were musical, if not honorable."

Debbie yawned and rubbed her eyes.

" I'll go and have a wash and get changed. God. My head feels like hell."

" Serves you right young lady. Coming home drunk, like that."

" I was not drunk, Mother. I knew exactly what I was doing all night."

" Good. Then it'll be on your own head if anything happens, won't it Lou, dear?"

Luke sniffed and grinned at Mo's expression as she rose.

Debbie looked at her with wide eyes.

" Mum. All we did was dance."

" Okay, love. Did I saw anything to the contrary?"

" You implied it."

" Must be your imagination, Love. Or guilt."

" We did not do anything else. Did we, Lou?"

" Nope."

" Okay, then. That's fine, isn't it. Now. I must get on and cook you some breakfast. I bet you're both ravenous?"

Debbie scowled at her Mother as she left the room and Luke grinned as he followed Mo into the kitchen, putting his cup in the sink.

He turned Mo to face him and kissed her lips lightly.

" I didn't touch her, Mo. Honest."

" I know, Lou. I was only teasin her."

She returned his kiss and moved away, her smile bright.

" I must say that you've certainly brought some sparkle back into this household, Lou."

" You and Derr is okay, ain't you?"

" As much as any married couple are after years of bein together, yeh. Oh. Derr's okay, he has his 'outside activities'. Nothing that I can do about that, Lou, it's the way of the world, I guess and I have accepted it. I think that he will be moving out soon now. I just get a bit frustrated at times, and, before you say anything, not like that, either. Mind. Oh. It doesn't matter."

Luke did not reply, and sat reading the paper until Debbie could be heard clattering around above them in her bedroom.

He excused himself and entered the bathroom, having, not only a good wash, but also a shave with Derrick's razor.

He returned to the kitchen to find his breakfast waiting for him and Debbie halfway through hers.

He winked at her and began to eat, realising just how hungry he actually was.

Afterwards, Luke and Debbie retired to the front room armed with fresh cups of coffee and continued to work on their songs, Debbie smiling over at Luke as she strummed quietly on her guitar.

" If I write the tunes can you put words to it, or do you work the other way round?"
" I'm easy either way, babe. I writes the words first normally, but I'll give it a go t'other way round if you like?"
" Good."
" Another ballad?"
" Oh, yes. I prefer them, don't you?"
" Yeh. Mostly, anyway."

Luke listened as Debbie hummed a simple tune, playing it over and over again. Luke found a blank cassette and put it in the machine as Debbie strummed and, as she began again, switched on the record button.

Afterwards, Luke took the machine over to the table and, as he played back Debbie's tune, began to write down several verses, changing a few line endings as he went.

Debbie was reading through some of her old notes as Luke slid the book over to her.

" Gosh. That was quick, Lou."
" See wot you thinks of it, the main part, anyway. We can harmonise on it later, too, if you like."

Debbie read through it swiftly, then re read it, humming the tune as she pointed at the words with her right forefinger.

" Lou. It's great. And the title, too. 'Key To My heart'. Wow. I'm impressed, Sir."

" That's just a title, we can change that it you wants to."

" No. No. It's all brill. The words give it the meaning. That's the right title for it. Oh, come on, Lou. Let's try it out, shall we?"

Debbie ran through it several times, altering the emphasis on a few of the words and smiled over at Luke with her eyebrows raised enquiringly.

" Well?"

" Baby, with you singin it, it's magic."

" Oh, come on Lou, be positive. Come on, "

Debbie leaned over and kissed Luke fully on the lips and smiled."

" I'm sober now, and it still feels as good. Lou, are you sure that you want to keep our friendship only on a professional level?"

" Yeh, be best, babe, for now, anyway."

" Okay. Right. Shall we put a longer intro and end to it? That will fill it out a little. I can chop and change the chords easily. What about you singing on it?"

" Wotever you think, Debs. I'll just clap at the end."

" Oh, Lou. You are the limit."

" Okay. I'll tap out the beat with me foot."

" Lou. That's it. Percussion. A simple drum beat. That's what we need. Drums."

" Yeh, and a lead guitar."

" Lou. I don't want to be in a rock band, thank you all the same."

" Sorry, babe."

" A soft drumbeat, that's what I want."

" I'll give you one."

" Excuse me?"

" Drum beat, woman, behave."

" Oh. We're still on a professional level then, are we?"

Luke simply glared at Debbie and she laughed, tossing her head and bending her lips to his once more.

" Hmm. This is more stimulating than coffee."

" Yeh, cheaper, too."

" Trust you to think of the cost."

" Let's go and get some drums then, babe."

" Just like that?"

" Yeh, why not. We needs them, so let's get them."

" And, I suppose, a guitar, too?"

" Well, yeh, now you mention it."

" Exactly, where, will we keep our equipment, and no funny cracks off you either, please, Lou?"

" We can rent somewhere, shouldn't be that friggin difficult."

" Lou."

" Yeh?"

" How long are you staying?"

" Dunno yet. Let's see how things goes, shall we, babe?"

Luke didn't want to get onto that topic right then and rose.

" Come on, let's go and see wot's about, shall we?"

Debbie came up to Luke and placed her arms around his shoulders and gently kissed his lips, probing him lightly with the tip of her tongue.

" Hmm. I hope that you stay forever, Lou."

As they were down town, Like and Debbie called into the estate agents, told them what they were looking for, but came away disappointed as nothing was available.

Debbie sounded genuinely sad.

" Oh, Lou. It's not going to be that easy after all, is it? We'll end up in some farmers field, I can see it."

" Hey, baby. That's it."

" What is?"

" Farmers. C'mon. I think I've cracked it."

Tommy Burton was standing on the back of a trailer shouting at some unfortunate lad who was fumbling with a sack of feed.

He grinned broadly as Luke emerged from the jaguar and shook his head.

" Hey, Lou. Wot's that, come with the job, does it?"

" Wot, the car or the bird?"

Debbie coughed lightly as she stood at his elbow.

" Bird, Lou?"

" Yeh. Sorry, Debs, figure of speech."

Tommy laughed.

" Figure, Lou. Only one that you knows about, I seem to recollect. You always was good at figures, haha. Anyway, wot can I do for you and your young lady? Hey, you bloody cretin. Wot the hell do you think you're doin, wastin feed like that."

The boy scurried away, trying to secure the end of the open hessian sack as corn dribbled from it in a steady stream.

Tommy bent down and accepted the smoke off Luke, breathing in heavily as Luke spoke.

" We're looking for somewhere to use, a shed or barn or somethin. Waterproof and in good nick, mind."

" What for, mate?"

" Store out musical instruments in and playin them. Writin songs, stuff like that."

" How big?"

" Oh. Any size really."

" Hmm. Nothin like that at all, Lou. I don't think I can...... No, hang on a bit. Fancy a cottage?"

" A cottage. Wot a house, type, thing?"

" Yeh. Pillock. You know Rosebank?"

" Yeh."

" Well, it's been empty now for nearly 18 months, since my old cowman left, and I got lumbered with these young arseholes that the labour exchange keeps sendin me."

" Is it dry?"

" Yeh, warm and cosy, too, for when you gets fed up of makin music. Haha, you can make hay while the Sun shines, then roll in it."

Debbie sniffed, but kept quiet.

" Can we see it?"

" Sure Lou. Wait there and I'll get you the keys."

Tommy soon returned, grinning as he handed the keys over to Luke.

" Tenner a week if you like it, do you okay?"

" Sure, Tommy. Cheers, mate."

Debbie literally flew out of the car as they pulled up outside the old, ivy- covered, property, her eyes shining as she took it all in.

" Oh, Lou. This is so wonderful. Come on, let's go inside, please."

She banged around from room to room, becoming more excited as she went.

" Oh, Lou. It will do, won't it? We'll be so happy here together, I know it."

" Hey, baby. It's a place to use, not to live in."

" I know, but it feels so homely. Can't you feel it?"

" Yeh. Feels comfortable and peaceful."

" Yes. Exactly. Oh, it's great."

After much discussion, they decided where their instruments would go, settling for the largest of the three bedrooms as it had a massive window which overlooked the flower- filled garden at the front, facing south to the open countryside towards Malvern and beyond.

It took them almost a week to assemble all of their gear together and, by the following weekend, Luke had set up his drums as he wanted them.

Debbie marvelled at the sheer size of it all, for, not only did Luke have five toms and a snare, but also, two tympanis, two bass drums five cymbals and a hi hat.

They had also bought an electric bass and a Stratocaster for general use and a semi acoustic Gibson for his blues work, together with 5 assorted amplifiers. Debbie chose the synthesizer and 16 channel mixing unit.

Luke was now lighter by some £8,000, but it was well worth it to him simply by the look of sheer pleasure on Debbie's face as she surveyed it all.

With the electricity now restored, they were all set to go, and both set about their tasks happi;y and full of energy.

Debbie carefully adjusted the microphone as she sat perched on a stool with her guitar across her knees and smiled over at Luke.

" Shall we try 'Key To My Heart' again, Lou. This time with a soft drum backing, Hi Hat and snare?"
" Yeh, okay, babe, let's get to it."
" After a kiss of course."

Luke shook his head as he crossed to her and pecked Debbie's cheek lightly.

" Is that all I get?"

Luke grinned widely and Debbie scowled.

" You know very well what I mean. God, Lou. Is that all you ever think of?"
" Wot?"
" You know. That."
" Wot's, that, when it's out?"
" Sex."
" Yeh, well. Helps the wheels turnin, don't it, baby?"

" If you say so, Lou. I must obviously be stuck in some mud somewhere, as my wheels are going nowhere fast. Now. Come here and let me show you what a kiss should be like."

Even Luke had to admit that he was aroused by Debbie's efforts but said nothing as he re-crossd to his drum kit, simply blowing out his cheeks and trying to ease his hard penis back down.

Luke was determined not to get involved with Debbie, but wondered how much longer they could stay as just friends? At least he would try, for now, at least.

They ran through the song several times and Debbie paused.

" I still think that we could improve it if we worked you in as a backing chorus, Lou?"

" Use the mixer?"

" Can we try it with you, just singing naturally, first, please? Come in at ' Can I tell you forever that I love you' at the same pitch as me. It's not too high for you, is it?"

" Dunno. I'll give it a whirl. I could try singin an octave down to harmonise with you?"

" Let's try it, anyway."

Luke switched on the recorder, gave a short roll on the drums and grinned at Debbie's pained expression.

Her guitar led them in and Luke fed a slow drum beat into it, watching her movements as Debbie started to sing.

Luke came in on each chorus line, dropping down an octave on the last two, leading out into the soft, slow, ending.

As they played it back, Luke nodded, half to himself.

" Yeh. Your voice is so damn good, Debs, you carry me along."

" Rubbish, Lou. It's 50- 50."

Again they played it through, Luke laying a slightly heavier beat down and, within an hour, they had it as they both liked it.

Luke picked up the Strat and flicked up and down the scales in a long, wailing, series of chords.

" Oh, Lou. I love that sound. I really wish that I could sing the blues, my voice just doesn't have the right qualities for it."

" Too sweet and angelic, babe."

" Huh. I don't know about that, Lou. Fancy a cup of coffee?"

" Cheers, babe."

Luke continued to play, singing quietly to his own version of 'Dimples' and Debbie clapped as he finished.

" Perhaps we ought to do a few bluesy ones? I'd love to have a go. Can you write something for me to try?"

" Sure, Deb. I'll have a crack at it."

She bent and kissed Luke tenderly on his lips before drifting away to the synthesizer, putting on the headphones as she experimented.

Luke set about writing the words, just simple arrangements which he altered to suit the style.

Luke titled it ' My Baby' and ran a few chords off on the guitar before switching the recorder on .

As they played it back, Debbie nodded.

" You are good, Lou. But will I be able to sing it okay, do you think?"

" Yeh. Just give it a go, Deb."

Luke let her play the opening chords on her acoustic before coming in with a steady, heavy, beat on one base, snare and Hi Hat.

The second time, Luke started the beat off on the synthesizer and picked up the Strat. He followed Debbie's high, clear, voice with a wailing 5th string lead, bending it to slide into each note as his fingers slid up and down the frets with practised ease.

When it was over, Debbie shook her head.

" No, Lou. I just can't get the right sound. It doesn't feel right to me. I feel that I ought to be screaming or growling it rather than singing it."

" Okay, babe. I'll sing it through, you fill in on the chorus."

Debbie nodded afterwards, a happy smile on her face.

" That was much better, Lou. I must try and get my voice to sounder rougher, don't you think?"

"We'll work on that, baby."

For another ten days they worked solidly, arriving before nine each morning and not leaving until after midnight for most of the time.

Derrick shrugged resignedly at Mo as they discussed it all, accepting that it was a working arrangement only between Luke and his Daughter, for the present, at least. Derrick did not really mind and, later that evening, he confirmed what Mo had already suggested would happen, that he would be leaving Mo soon to live with his other woman in his life. Luke said nothing, simply congratulating Derrick, but at trhe same time feeling sad for Mo, who was losing her man after all these years.

The following Friday they went to another dance, meeting up with Debbie's friends. They were all fascinated to learn what she and Luke were doing and made her promise to let them all come and listen to them soon, doing some of Debbie's 'Blondie' numbers. Luke was unaware that she did any, and looked forward to hearing these for himself, gazing at Debbie with new admiration.

As they all chatted at the bar, Luke spotted Ruth weaving across towards them, her face beaming.

" Hi, Lou."
" Hi baby. We meets again?"
" Yeh. By yourself?"
" More or less, yeh."
" Oh. You poor thing. I'll buy you that drink I promised you now, if you like?"
" Yeh. Cheers, babe."

As she paid for them and handed the brimming glass over, Ruth grinned up at Luke.

" Borin here, ain't it?"
" Aw. It ain't too bad, girl."
" Not so lively as the last one, for you, anyway?"

" Yeh, well. We don't want that too often, does we?"

Ruth didn't answer and only gazed at Luke as he offered her a smoke after lighting them both.

" Where's Manda?"
" Oh. She's over with the mob. Can't you hear her, noisy cow that she is?"

She pointed and Luke saw her amongst some twenty or so laughing and shouting people over near one of the walls.

" Come over and join us, Lou?"
" Naw. I'll leave it out, babe. Don't ,mind, does you?"
" Yeh. I do."

She giggled at Luke.

" I'll see you later then, perhaps?"
" Yeh. Never know your luck, babe, does you?"

Debbie materialized at his shoulder.

" A friend?"
" Yeh. Daughter of one of me old mates."

" Oh. Like me, you mean?"

" Yeh. Not in your league, Debs. C'mon, baby. Let's get you on the floor."

" Pardon?"

" Fuckin hell, Debs. Dancin, you pillock."

" Oh. Yes. And I am not a pillock. If you spoke properly, we'd have a lot less confusion, wouldn't we, dear?"

" Yeh. Be more borin though, wouldn't it, deary?"

They danced as the record thundered out and Luke rested against the wall as it finished, listening to the DJ.

" And now, folks, it's smoochy time. We'll kick off with a dedication to two of my old friends, Lou and Debbie. Here's Chicago telling us that ' You're The Inspiration'. Get to it, both."

Luke reached for Debbie and they came together on the dance floor as the music started. As they danced, Debbie sang softly in his ear, sending Luke's senses higher and higher, as her lips rested lightly against his skin.

' You know our love was meant to be, from tonight until forever' Luke began to whisper the words back to her and, all too soon, the song was over and the spell broken as reality returned.

Breaking apart, Debbie picked up her drink and pointed to his.

" Come on, Lou, my turn."

He followed her to the bar and waved to her friends to follow, treating them all as they gathered eagerly around.
Debbie shook her head afterwards.

" You're too good to them, Lou."
" Friends of yours, baby, is friends of mine."
" They're your friends too, Lou,. Don't forget that."

Debbie finished her drink and threw her arms tightly around Luke's shoulders.

" Oh. I feel so happy tonight, Lou. Think I'll go onto cider next."
" Jeez."
" Oh. Don't worry. I won't have that much. Still, you can always carry me home, eventually, couldn't you, afterwards?"
" Afterwards, wot?"
" You tell me. You're the expert, Lou"

The dance progressed and the drinks flowed for them all and Luke held Debbie tightly as, yet another, ballad pulsed out from the stage.

Debbie rested her head on Luke's shoulders, alternating humming along to the tune and kissing his lips.

Yet another round was bought, and they came together once more as Phil Collin's 'Against All Odds' started.

Debbie's eyes were closed and she sighed deeply, happy within his arms.

Luke kissed her cheek gently, nuzzling down to her neck with his lips. She moaned softly and pushed her neck against his warm, waiting, lips and sighed again.

With his tongue, Luke flicked it up to her ear, staying there for a few moments, before he moved on, brushing against her parted lips.

" Oh, Lou."

Their kiss was long, full of tender feeling and emotion, and accompanied by loud cheers and clapping as they finally broke from it.

Debbie gazed deeply into Luke's eyes.

" Lou. Why does this always happen at dances? This magical feeling between us?"

" Dunno, babe, perhaps it's the booze?"

122

" Lou. Are we really only friends. Don't I mean any more to you than that?"

" Baby, c'mon, let's just enjoy it, shall we? Yeh, course you means a lot to me, you is special, Debs. I just wants it this way, for now, at least."

He kissed her deeply once more and held Debbie close to him, knowing that he really did want her if he was truthful.

Luke pulled away and lit up another smoke, giving one of their friends a light also.

Taking up the offer of another drink, Luke followed them all to the bar. Even Luke was beginning to feel well topped up and, as he gazed at his companions noticed that most were already over their limit, including most of the girls who were laughing and tittering over at one end of the bar together.

He saw that Debbie was laughing along with them, guessing that the oldest among them was no more than 22 or 23 and grinned inwardly, accepting his drink. As Debbie came forward to claim her refill, she poked out her tongue at Luke as he winked at her, still laughing at some joke that her friend was telling.

Luke listened to the talk as he rejoined the young men, noticing that the discussion was about motor bikes.

He mentioned a few British bike makes but, to his disgust, only one had heard of them.

Out of the corner of his eye Luke saw a youth standing talking to Debbie. He stood with his head close to hers and Luke saw that Debbie's face was flushed and angry now.

One of the group tried to draw Luke's attention back but he kept his eyes on her.

Dave, one of the youths, spoke, laughing.

" It'll be okay, Lou. That's her boyfriend. Ex boyfriend, I should say."

" Didn't know she had one."

" Oh. Didn't you? She ain't seen him for months now. We thought he'd moved away."

Luke felt a sharp pain in his back and he shot forward into the group, spilling his drink over one of them.

" Oi. You."

Luke concentrated on saving the remainder of his pint.

" You okay?"

" Yeh. It's okay, Lou. Ignore him."

" Yeh, balls to him. I ain't fightin him over Debs."

" Hey, you. I want you."

A hand now grabbed Luke's shoulder and he turned round to face Debbie's, obviously not, ex, boyfriend.

He was quite a well-built youth, but soft and flabby, as well as being inexperienced, and Luke shook his head slowly.

" Look. Piss off, mate, will you. You've cost me a drink already."

" What''s this about you and Debbie?"

" Wot about us?"

" Lay off her. Okay?"

" say's who?"

" Say's me. Right, fuckhead?"

" Or else?"

" Or else I push your fuckin face in, you middle aged cunt. Okay?"

Luke digested this slowly as all of his friends held their breath, waiting for the explosion to come.

Luke simply shrugged.

" You goin out with her, then, yeh?"

" Yeh. I was, and I will be again. Okay?"

Luke turned his eyes towards Debbie.

" That right, Debs?"

His voice carried over to her as she stood, stock still, and terrified.

" You goin out with him, or were you?"

She nodded ever so slightly, sending tresses of her hair over her face and Luke saw the tears glistening in her eyes.

" Why didn't you tell me?"

Debbie simply lifted up her shoulders and let them fall in a sad, dejected, manner.

The youth spoke again, his voice and stance total arrogance.

" Satisfied now, arsehole?"

" Yeh. If that's the way she wants it, that's okay with me."

" You ain't got no fuckin choice, grand dad."

Luke merely turned and walked away, knowing that he would seriously injure the mouth if he stayed a second longer.

Luke strode out through the crowded dance hall, ignoring them all, and the gleaming Jaguar shot like a bullet along the road, hardly slowing down until he roared into the Falcon car park in a flurry of gravel and smoking tyres.

It was 10.45pm and a dance was in full swing here, too, the band playing a very loud waltz.

Luke sat on a vacant stool at the bar, his face set like thunder.

" Well. Hello, stranger. Who's rattled your cage, then?"

" Hi Sally. Give us a pint of Guinness, babe, please."

Luke paid for it this time, silencing her with a wave of his hand.

" Want one, babe?"

" Well. Okay, while we've a few spare minutes, I will. Cheers."

" You're welcome."

Luke took one of Sally's cigarettes, offering her a light as she eyed him carefully.

" Has something upset you, Lou?"

" Yeh. Sort of, babe. Forget it. Okay?"

" If you say so. Look. I'll have to go now as we're really rushed. We've an extension, too.

" Okay. Catch you again, Sall."

" Stick around, if you like."

" Yeh. Need a hand?"

" Not really. Unless you fancy washing glasses?"

" Suits me."

" Okay. I'll close this bar soon, it'll be quieter for you then."

Luke lifted the bar flap with old familiarity and began to swill out the stacked glasses.

One or two wanted refills and Luke served them, finally figuring out how to operate the new till.

Around 11.10pm Luke turned off the bar lights, locking the door of the back bar. Those who remained moved off into the middle lounge or front bar and Luke collected the empties from the tables, stacking them carefully on the, already crowded, bar.

Sally squeezed past Luke as he washed up, a small grin on her flushed face.

" I think we're winning, Lou."

He moved carefully out of the way as she dragged a full case of Forest Browns out from beneath the counter.

" Yeh. Let's hope so."

Sally shot away again, her arms full of bottles and Luke continued to wash and polish the glasses.

One of the barmaids deposited another full tray of dirty glasses beside him, taking a tray of clean ones away with her and Luke sighed as he began on them.

By midnight, he had beaten it and the few that remained he washed at a more leisurely pace.

Sitting on one of the stools in the darkened bar, Luke lit up a smoke, resting his arms on the bar top as he took in a deep lungful.

" For you, Lou."

Sally plonked a brimming pint before him. She sipped at her own drink and took one of Luke's cigarettes, using his lighter also.

"Whew. These do's get worse by the month. Either that, or I'm getting old."

" Ain't we all, babe?"

" Oh. I say. You are bloody cheerful tonight?"

" Yeh. Well, it happens sometimes."

" You should be so lucky."

" Haha. Okay, Sal. Let's say I got took for a sucker."

" By a certain young lady?"

" Yeh."

" Ah. I see."

" I wish I did. Pain in the arse."

" Who, her, or women in general?"
" Yeh."

Luke sighed heavily as he stubbed out his dog end.

" Any chance of a room here, Sal?"
" Bad as that, eh?"
" Yeh. I'm stayin at her folk's place."
" Haha. Oh. I like it, Lou. Dangerous ground, that. Yes, of course you can have a room. I've a couple spare."
" Okay. But I'll pay you now, in case I goes early."
"Lou."
" Listen. You has to make a livin. So, no crap about not payin, okay?"
" Okay, Lou. You win. Are you staying around Bromyard, then?"
" Dunno yet, Sal. I'll see how things goes."
" Oh well. Fancy a bite to eat, then. There's loads of grub left?"
" Wot, tomorrow's dinner?"
" Ha. Found out at last. No. It's no fun though these days, trying to make ends meet."
" You looks well on it anyway, babe."
" Ha. You must be getting back to normal?"
" Wot?"
" Compliments."
" I don't usually compliment no one."

" So I noticed, Lou. While the rest of the male population are trying to chat me up with a load of bull, you simply sit back and laugh at me, or ignore me with your eyes."

" Who?"

" You do. Anyway, I'm off to get a bite to eat. Do you want yours in here?"

" Yeh. Please."

Some minutes later Sally brought back a tray full of sandwiches, laying them down on the bar between them. She dropped a key into his hand and chuckled.

" Number six. Okay. Don't wake up the others as you stomp up the stairs."

" That friggin band should keep them awake."

" They've nearly finished now. Not going up for a waltz then, Lou?"

" Huh. Hey. I will if you will."

" Oh yes. I bet you would, too?"

" I'm serious, babe. That'd make them talk. Bang goes your reputation."

" What reputation? Any lady that keeps a pub doesn't have a reputation. Well, she does, in one sense."

" Did you say, lady?"

" Okay, scruff. Keep it buttoned. God. Can you imagine it if you trotted in there in your tee shirt and jeans, long hair and earring, not to mention your tattoo's? Oh. Come on, Lou, let's do it quickly before I change my mind and regret it for the rest of my life."

Sally dragged him through the bar, up the stairs and onto the dance floor.

There were still many couples dancing, the men wearing suits and the ladies long dresses.

Sally took hold of Luke and they moved out gracefully among them. Round and round they went, drawing odd looks from several dancers, who gave each other knowing nods and winks when they saw Sally.

She giggled up at him.

" Silly cows. I bet they stay up all night talking about me."

Luke held her close and bent his head to Sally's ear.

" Hey. I wants a pee."

She collapsed against him, her deep laugh bursting out.

" Oh. Oh. Lou. You bloody idiot. Do you, really?"
" Naw. Just windin you up, babe."

They laughed together and continued around the room.

When the dance ended, Sally curtsied to him demurely as Luke bowed to her before they ran from the room arm in arm, laughing loudly.

By 1.30am the staff had gone home and the dance floor was empty and locked.

Sally went around all of the outside doors and windows, checking that they were all locked and secure before returning to the bar to empty the tills.

After it was all counted, Luke helped Sally take it into the office and lock it away in the floor safe.

Sally sighed as the safe door was locked again.

" Oh. I'm always so glad when that's done."

" Ever been blagged?"

" Pardon?"

" Robbed."

" Oh. No. But I'm always fearful of it. Coffee, Lou?"

" Yeh. Cheers, Sal."

" Come on. Then I'm off to bed. Big day, Saturday, everyone wants the day off."

" I'll lend you a hand if you like."

" Just like the old days for you here, isn't it, Lou?"

" Yeh. Sort of."

" Okay. I really do appreciate your offer, Lou. But you really must let me pay you properly."

" Properly?"

" Yes. Why the funny grin?"

" Aw. It's an expression that always makes me smile."

" Happy days?"

" Yeh. Definitely."

" Was she pretty?"

" The best."

" Still, after all these years?"

" Oh yeh."

" Were you worse or better in those days, Lou?"

" Depends wot at, babe."

Sally laughed lightly and passed Luke his coffee, giving him a broad smile.

" Well, sir. I'm off to bed. I'll see you in the morning, then?"

" Yup. I'm off to kip meself now. See you, babe."

Luke came down the following morning to find the cleaners busily eliminating all trace of the previous evening's existence and quickly passed through to the street to buy some razor blades and foam, as all of his stuff was still at Debbie's, and he had no intention of facing her today.

As he sat down in the dining room to a breakfast prepared by Sally herself, Luke glanced over at her as she sat nibbling her toast and opening the mail.

" It's always blasted bills and circulars. They must spend a fortune on junk mail. I ask you. Why the hell should I need a new, miracle, deaf aid? Or, for that matter, thermal underwear? And no comments off you, either, thank you, Lou."

Luke just grinned as he sipped his coffee.

" Wot's on today then, boss?"
" Plenty. Believe me."
" Good. The more the better."
" Well. At least you look a bit more placid today. Did you sleep well?"
" Yeh. I waltzed through it."
" Oh. Haha. Yes. That was fun, I must say."
" Yeh. We'll have to do it again."
" Will we now? Just remember, I'm the boss here."
" Oh. Yeh. Sorry, your bossiness."

Luke set about his tasks willingly, it soon all coming back to him and, before Sally had even asked him to, Luke had restocked the shelves and put on a new barrel of bitter for the back bar.

Sally was impressed and left him to it as Luke swept the yard. Sally reappeared, her face flushed.

" Oh. What did I say? Now, my dear, sweet, Saturday girl has called in sick. She's kitchen staff, so, rather than ask you to wait at table, which I'm sure you would do admirably, can I ask you to cover the back bar for me?"

" Sure, babe. No sweat. I might spill the soup if I doles out the nosh."

" Yes. I'm sure that you would, and not altogether accidently either, knowing you? You'd probably end up telling the customers to hurry up, too. I often feel like that myself sometimes."

Luke sat behind the bar reading through the newspaper having served what few customers there were that early in the day.

It started to fill up around midday and Luke was soon flat out serving once more.

One or two of Debbie's friends from the night before came in also, Luke remembering Dave.

" Hi, mate."

" Oh. Hi, Lou. Workin here now?"

" Yeh. Keeps me out of trouble."

" Want one, too?"

" Cheers, Dave. Bottle of Guiness will do nicely, thanks. How's things goin?"

" Okay."

" Dance okay last night?"

" Yeh. You should have stayed, Lou."

" Naw."

Dave moved away to join his friends and Luke did some washing up between serving customers.

When Dave returned for a refill, Luke paid for the round, watching Dave closely as he hesitated at the bar, obviously uncertain of whether to speak or not.

" Lou. About Debbie and Terry."

" Look, mate. I ain't interested, okay. I don't like bein taken for a ride."

" How?"

" Her and him. She never even mentioned she had a fuckin boyfriend."

" That's cos she didn't, then."

" But she has now?"

" No, not really. Look. Terry's a pratt and will soon piss off again, this time, for good, I hope."

" I still ain't interested, Dave. Leave it, okay?"

" Sure, Lou, if you say so."

As Dave took the tray of glasses over to the table, his companions all raised their drinks to him and Luke nodded absently, his thoughts elsewhere. They drifted to Debbie, why had she not told him about this ex boyfried, especially if she was still interested in him? It made no sense to Luke, as Debbie had been the one making all of the running in their relationship, wanting more than simple friendship off him.

The afternoon passed quickly enough and, at last, they were closed and eating dinner.

" I see wot you mean about bein busy, Sall?"

" Lou. That wasn't busy, believe me. Wait until tonight. Do you want a job tonight, as one of the girls from the bar will help me in the kitchen?"

" Sure. I'm happy in the back bar."

" What about the front?"

" Yeh, suppose so. I'm happier in the back though, but will help out there, too, if you wants?"

" Thanks, Lou. You are an angel, do you know that?"

" Yeh. But wot sort, babe?"

" God. That was a long time ago, Lou, you and the hell's angels?"

" Yeh. Don't you start remindin me, neither, Sall."

The evening started quietly enough, but built up to a packed house by a little after 8.00pm. The lounge bar was the same and Luke was kept extremely busy pulling pints here, there and everywhere. He had to change, yet another, barrel and fit two new optics up and he paused to survey the packed bars. The smoke was thick in the large back bar and the juke box thundered out non-stop, Luke having turned it up after several requests.

Luke didn't notice Debbie at first as she was sat in a corner, only recognizing her boyfriend, Terry, when he came across for a drink..

Luke served him, civility at a minimum as he glanced at Terry's grinning face.

' He really thinks he's it." Luke thought to himself

Dave and the rest came in then and Luke treated them all once more.

Dave offered Luke a smoke and grinned.

" Bloody busy, ain't it?"
" Too true, mate. This'll keep me fit."
 Ha. Yeh. You look fuckin well fit enough to me,

Lou."

Manda, Ruth and their group came in then and Luke was kept busy, avoiding Ruth's enquiring eyes as best he could as she glanced at him, then Debbie, then back to Luke.

Ruth sat herself down at the end of the bar next to the jukebox, settled for the night, Luke thought.

She spoke to him at every available opportunity, offering Luke smokes and helping herself to his, which he had left on the bar top.

Ruth put Jim Diamond on the jukebox and, as ' I Sleep Alone At Nights' came on, smiled over at Luke.

" I like this one, don't you, Lou?"
" Yeh. S'okay, ain't it. Want another drink, babe?"
" Yeh. Thanks, Lou."

Luke returned to her end of the bar whenever he could, noticing Debbie on several occasions as she glanced in his direction.

Luke's eyes didn't linger on hers, and he served Terry in silence when he came up for refills.

Ruth held her empty glass up for him and he grinned.

" You like your cider, don't you?"
" Yeh. It's only my third glass though."
" Okay. This'll make two pints."
" It's good for you."
" Oh yeh?"
" It's true."
" Hang on, babe."

Luke had to serve another group and, when he returned to her, Ruth was ready for a refill.

" Fuckin hell, babe. Why don't you drink pints?"
" Okay. I will."
" You're jokin?"
" Nope. I'm not. I'll have a pint this time, barman."

Luke placed the full pint down in front of her.

" On me, Ruth."
" Cheers, Lou. Cheap night for me, this."
" How old is you, babe?"
" Old enough, Lou, believe me."
" Yeh? But is you eighteen?"

She picked up her drink and sipped it, winking at Luke over the brim.

Luke grinned and washed a few glasses up. 'You're The Inspiration' came on and Luke looked up, but it wasn't Debbie putting it on. As it started, Debbie, too, looked up, but soon dropped her gaze as Terry tightened his arm around her shoulders, bending his head to hers.

Ruth smiled at Luke, her glass almost empty once more.

" See. It don't take long to empty it, does it, Lou?"

" It ain't empty yet."
" It is now."

Ruth set the glass down heavily as she swallowed the last of its contents.

" You never wants another one, babe, does you?"
" Why not?"
" Jeez. Okay, comin up."

Ruth seemed to slow down after that, and Luke topped it up with half pints each time.

By now Luke could see that she was well steamed and she gazed over at him with dreamy eyes, talking to him whenever he came near. Ruth ignored everyone else and sat, swaying to the music as it belted out.

Every time that Ruth went to the toilet Luke noticed that she came back a little more unsteadily than the last time, and, finally, she almost fell off her stool, Luke's arm alone saving her.

Ruth clung to his hand.

" Thanks, Lou. I think that this be my last pint."

She lifted the half empty glass and drank it swiftly, Luke managing to catch it before it slammed into the bar as she brought it down hard.

The front bar had now eased up a little, so the barmaid helped Luke out when required and he noticed that Ruth was drinking again.

" Wot the hell's that?"
" Vodka."
" Fuckin hell, babe."
" I like it. I've gone off pints for tonight."

Terry came over once more for refills and Luke began to fill the order.
Looking hard at Ruth, Terry sneered.

" Pissed again?"
" Wot's it to you?"
" Nothin. Just sayin. You look a right tramp, you know that?"
" Piss off."
" Yeh. I am. I'll leave you to who you deserve."

Luke ignored this taunt at him and took the money without speaking.
Terry had drunk over his limit and baited Luke further.

" I heard that you were supposed to be some sort of hard case. But it don't seem that way to me."

Luke shrugged, not speaking.

" Is my change right?"
" Yeh."
" Oh. It fuckin well speaks. Well, Ruth's more your match. She's always pissed and you're full of it."

Luke looked hard at the bar top before turning away to move some bottles.
Ruth's slurred voice rang out.

" I wouldn't let him talk to you like that, Lou. I'm not always pissed, anyway."

Terry rocked on his heels and shouted for all the bar to hear.

" Shut up you fuckin drunken whore."

Ruth stepped down from her stool and tottered over to his table as he continued.

" Piss off you scrubber."
" I'm not, and you know it. You've tried often enough, and lately, last week, remember down the cemetery?"
" Fuck off, whore."

" I am not."

Ruth accompanied the last word by throwing one of the drinks directly into Terry's face.

Luke saw the startled look as the liquid burnt into his face and he also saw Ruth fly backwards and collapse onto the floor in a silent heap as Terry's clenched fist struck her on the side of her head.

With a roar, Luke vaulted the bar and was on him. Terry tried desperately to defend himself, but it was all over in a matter of seconds as Terry slumped sidewards on the bench seat as Luke struck him a savage chop to the neck.

Dragging him through the crowded bar by his legs, Luke propped open the door and threw Terry, bodily, down the stone steps, turning to an ashen-faced Dave,

" When that mother-fucker wakes up tell him, from me, that if I even smell him anywhere near Bromyard, then I'm comin after him to finish him off. Got that, Dave?"

" Yeh. Yeh, okay, Lou."

Luke bent and gently lifted the, now moaning, Ruth up from the floor, pushing through the crowd. He carried through the front bar and up the stairs into his room, laying her gently down on his bed.

" You okay, babe?"

"Oh. My head. My head."

" Look. Stay here for a while, Ruth. I'll come back later. You sure you're okay?"

" Apart from a sore head. He hit me, Lou. He hit me. Oh. I need a drink."

" Christ, girl. There's some over there, but go easy, okay?"

" Yeh. I will."

Luke hurried back downstairs. Debbie was sitting bolt upright in the corner as Dave talked to her.

Luke ignored them both and went back behind the bar to serve the waiting customers.

Terry had been carried off out of the way, Dave told him as Luke refilled their glasses.

" Lay off him, Lou. You'll kill him."

" He don't think so."

" He's a fuckin fool, Lou. All mouth and no action. How's Ruth?"

" She'll be okay. I ought to finish that bastard off right now for wot he did to her. Was it true wot Ruth was sayin about him tryin it on with her, do you think?"

" That's wot Deb was askin just. I reckon it was, yeh, knowin him. He thinks he's so fuckin irresistible to women."

Luke gazed over at Debbie as she sat staring sadly down at the table top before her.

" Come and speak to her, Lou, she's really upset."

" No way, mate, she chose that arsehole, she can sort it."

The jukebox soon boomed out once more and the next time that Luke looked, Debbie and some of her friends had left.

He also noticed that Manda and Co had gone, but didn't remember seeing them for a long time.

Dave, too, waved a goodbye as the rest of his group left and, at last, Luke locked the back bar door with a sigh of relief, as he began to wash up the empty glasses.

It was 12.40am when he finally went upstairs to bed, leaving Sally sorting paperwork in her office.

Ruth was lying on her side on the bed, her coat in a heap on the floor.

Luke picked it up and she opened her eyes.

" Lou. Lou. Wassa time?"

" Nearly quarter to one. How do you feel now?"

" Horrible."

" Do you want me to run you home?"

" I'll stay here, Lou."

" You can't."

" Why not?"

" Sally might find you."

" Why, is she comin in here, too?"

She tittered drunkenly and tipped the brandy bottle up to her lips.

" S'nearly all gone, Lou."

" That was half full when I left."

" Must have a leak in it then. Oh, Lou. I'm too comfy to move."

Ruth stretched herself out on the bed and Luke set the bottle down carefully.

Sitting down next to her, she gazed at him blankly.

" Put the light out, Lou. It's too bright."

To save an argument, Luke rose and, after flicking the switch, returned to her on the bed.

"Oh.That'better, Lou."

Her hand found his and she squeezed it.

" Don't I turn you on?"

" You're pissed, Ruth."

" I'm not that pissed, believe me."

Ruth pulled Luke down to her and gave him a long and passionate kiss.

" There. Am I pissed or not?"
" Well, babe, I ain't quite sure now, babe."

Luke grinned down at her in the dark as they came together again. This time, their hands moved over each other.

Ruth wasn't a virgin, Luke soon found that out, but she wasn't that experienced either and, when they were both lying naked on the bed, Luke proceeded to get to work on her eager body. Whether it was because of the drink or not, Ruth didn't take long to arouse and she was gasping and moaning even as he slid slowly into her.

Their love-making lasted a good hour, after which, Luke had persuaded Ruth to go home.

Helping her, they crept down the stairs and out of the back door, watched by an amazed Sally.

" I'll explain it all later, Sall, I promise."

He grinned feebly and helped Ruth into his car.

She demanded that they make love once more before he took her home, so he pulled up in a gateway and took her again, finally depositing at her gate at 4.10am.

Sally was nowhere around when Luke returned to the Falcon and he crept thankfully up to his bed.

As it was a Sunday, Luke didn't come downstairs until almost 10.00am, finding Sally already busy bustling about.

Seeing him, she broke off answering one of the cleaner's questions and crossed to Luke, wasting no time in coming to the point.

" Lou. I don't want to appear as if I'm interfering, but, I don't expect you to turn this place into a knocking shop. That's just the ammunition that the busy-bodies around here need against me."

" Hey. It wasn't like that, Sall. She was the girl hurt in the fight last night in the back bar."

" What fight? It's the first that I've heard about it."

Luke explained briefly, concluding.

" And I was takin her home when you saw us."

" Hmm. And you didn't invite her up there for any other reason?"

" Nope. She wasn't quite conscious when I carried her up."

" Conscious, or sober?"

" Yeh, wotever. There was enough people about, babe."

" Okay, Lou. I believe you. I'm sorry for snapping at you."

" S'okay boss. I'm your servant, after all."

" You'll be something else if you don't shut up."

" Hey, promises, baby."

" I'll give you, baby, in a minute."

" Wot?"

" You heard, and don't try and twist it round, either, youngster."

" Ha. I'll give you a few years, Sall."

" You reckon?"

" Yeh. Ten, at least."

" Oh. Come on, Lou. You can't be serious?"

" I am. Come on, how old is you?"

" I'm not telling you that, am I?"

" You don't ever seem to tell me nothin, girl."

" Why should I?"

" Oh. No reason."

" Perhaps, one day, I might."

The telephone rang and Sally came back, a smile on her face.

" A young lady for you."

" Who?"

" God. I'm not your slave, Lou, you know. Carol, I think."

Picking up the receiver, Luke found that It was one of Debbie's friends.

" Lou. Is it okay if Deb gets her stuff from the cottage?"
" Yeh. Sure, but tell her she can still use the place if she wants."
" Okay, Lou. I've a message from her, too."
" I don't want to know, okay?"
" Sure, and, thanks."

Sally stood with an inquisitive look as he put down the receiver.

" Is this the reason why you're here?"
" Partly, yeh."
" What's the other reason?"
" You said I could be."
" Don't be flippant."
" Whoo. The other reason is cos I wants to be."
" Oh no. Not you as well?"
" Wot?"
" Getting all sloppy."
" Jeez. Naw. S'only cos of your cookin, girl. I feels safer with you anyway, like, cos of your age."

" Oh, Lou. You are such a blasted idiot. Come on then, I'll fix us some breakfast."

" Brill. Hey, I don't want your money and, if you're that old, I certainly don't want your body."

" Old? You certainly know the way to a girls heart, don't you?"

" Oh yeh. Lot's of practise, babe."

Opening time came and Luke covered both bars until Sally emerged to take over the front from him, looking, to his eye, extremely lovely in a deep, crimson, velvet calf-length dress and silver chain belt.

Sally smiled at him, her eyes bright.

" What's the matter, Lou?"

" Aw. Nothin, babe. I just thought, naw, s'okay."

Luke turned away from her quizzical stare and busied himself with the shelves. Soon the back began to fill up with the regulars. Among them Dave and a few more of Debbie's gang, including Carol, who grinned at him over the bar.

" I gave Deb your message, Lou."

" Cheers, babe. Have this one on me."

Dave offered the smokes around and lit Luke's from his lighter.

" Won't you even listen to Debbie's message, Lou?"

" Nope. I don't like getting shit on."

" Lou. That's just it, though."

" Look. Leave it, Dave, yeh? I don't want to fall out with you, okay?"

"Yeh. Okay, Lou."

Trade was brisk for the rest of opening time and Luke thankfully locked the doors at 2.20pm. He washed up and, as Sally was busy with guests, left quietly for the cottage.

Chapter 5

He collected the Strat and one of the amplifiers, noticing that Debbie stuff was still there. He picked up Debbie's guitar, laying it gently back down once more as he sighed.

After listening to a tape of her lovely voice, Luke left the cottage with mixed emotions and a regret that he just couldn't quite put his finger on.

Back at the Falcon, Luke carried the guitar and amp up into the deserted ballroom and, after plugging them in, began to play softly to himself.

Running through the tunes, Luke kept coming back to the one that Debbie had made up for ' Key To My Heart' and he hummed the words.

Sally arrived with two cups of coffee and a plate of sandwiches, placing them gently on the stage as she sat beside him, listening quietly without speaking.

" Oh. Don't stop. I think that's great. I hope that you don't mind me coming in?"

" Course not, Sall."

" I like all sorts of music."

" Yeh? Wot about this?"

Luke played several blues intro's and Sally smiled, her face bright.

" Oh, Blues. I simply adore that. God. That brings back some memories."

" You like Blues?"

" Don't look so amazed, Lou. I wasn't always a pub landlady, you know."

" Yeh?"

" Yes. I used to play once, myself."

" Blues?"

" No. More conventional, I'm afraid, though I did try a few bluesy-type tunes to myself."

Luke handed the Strat to her and Sally grinned.

" I've never played an electric one before, Lou."

" Okay, I'll knock off the wellie channel for you. Sound more natural then."

" Really, how fascinating."

Sally took the guitar carefully from him and picked up a spare plectrum.

As she played, Luke laughed.

" Hey, babe. I've never heard that played on a Strat before."

" You know it?"

156

" Yeh. Part of Bach's Brandenburg Concerto Number 4."

" Good God. You never cease to amaze me. No. Really, I should have expected this off you. You're not the brainless thug that you make yourself out to be, are you?"

" Oh, cheers, Sall."

" You know very well what I mean."

" Yeh. So, you were a classical head-banger, was you?"

" Yes. I'm afraid so. How's that wellie channel of yours work?"

Luke pressed the pedal with his foot and Sally tried out a few blues-cum-Bach chords, laughing as she put down the guitar.

" Oh. I can't get the hang of that. Isn't the action really smooth and fast?"

" Yeh. Has to be, you get into some pretty hectic finger work sometimes."

" What was that one that you were playing when I came in, Lou?"

" Oh. A little somethin that me and a friend knocked up.

" Play it again for me, Lou, please."

Luke dropped the distortion a little and played it through. Then, he repeated it, this time, singing the words quietly.

Sally clapped when he finished.

" That was really lovely. Who wrote the words?"

" Me."

" Did you really? Who wrote the tune?"

" My friend."

" It's a nice tune, too. Have you written anymore together?"

" Yeh. A few."

Luke played through some of the others before straying into some blues again, then, putting down the guitar, he finished off his coffee and munched on a beef and Horseradish sandwich.

Sally was obviously impressed and smiled at him.

" What else can you do, musically?"

" Oh. This and that, not a lot really."

" I can't believe that of you, Lou, you're not the modest type."

" Hey. You getting at me again, Sall?"

" Haha."

" How did you get into music then, Sall. Was you in an orchestra?"

" Yes. A youth orchestra, but I dropped out after a while."

Her eyes looked far away and Luke grinned.

" Young and in love, was you?"
" Pardon? No, Lou. Why?"

Sally actually blushed then and turned hurriedly away from him to study floral pattern on the far wall.

" Did it work out okay in the end, though?"

Sally didn't answer and Luke went on.

" I guess not, cos you're here, ain't you? If it's anythin like my life, Sall, you've had your fill of things, ain't you, good and bad?"

Sally turned slowly, tears glistening in her eys.

" Still love him, does you, babe?"

She nodded slightly.

" Can't you get in touch with him, Sall?"
" He. He's dead."

" Jeez. I'm sorry, babe. He'd have been one lucky sod to have had you, too."

She broke into a flood of tears then and Luke reached forward, pulling Sally to him.

She clung to him tightly, sobbing loudly into his shoulders and Luke stroked the back of her neck and kissed her fragrant hair gently, deciding that Sally was really quite beautiful this close up.

Her eyes searched his and Luke smiled tenderly.

" I knows wot you feels like, Sall, believe me."
" Do you? Do you really, Lou?"
" Yeh. I, well. A long time ago, I lost…"

His voice dropped to a whisper and halted.

" Did you lose someone close to you?"
" Yeh. My little bright eyes. Hazel, her name was. She was so kind and gentle, never hurt no one in the world. She was so beautiful in every way. She was pregnant when she died. She died of Leukemia before givin birth."
" Oh Lou. I'm so terribly sorry, I really am."
" Aw. It was over twenty years ago now, babe."
" Is she buried here, in Bromyard?"
" Yeh. I still visits their grave."

160

They both had tears in their eyes now and they embraced tightly once more, neither speaking.

Eventually, Sally's muffled voice reached him.

" Mike was killed in a plane crash in Greece. He was a pilot. I was devastated. We were going to be married too. Ever since then, I've kept away from men."

" You serious?"

" Yes. I am. They don't interest me at all. They all seem to be out for one thing. Perhaps I misjudged a few but, by and large, they are all the same to me."

Luke took Sally's head in his hands and gazed deeply into her dark brown eyes.

" I think that you is a beautiful and lovely person, Sal, really I does. No bullshit."

Luke kissed her tenderly, feeling her tension.

Sally's lips were sweet and full and Luke kissed her deeply once more.

Although her lips parted a little, she responded no more.

Luke drew away and smiled.

" This is as a friend then, okay?"

Her wide eyes were still tear-bright and Luke touched his lips to them before returning to hers.

Sally was soon responding to him with a hungriness that startled him at first, but he soon matched it, and they swayed together on the edge of the stage as Sally's tongue finally sought his out.

Sally pulled Luke to her and planted kisses on his cheek and neck as she blindly sought him with tightly closed eyes.

Luke led her, trembling, across the deserted dance floor and closed his bedroom door behind them.

As he sat her on the bed, Luke kissed Sally once more, soon bringing all of his passions to the surface.

As she lay back, Luke began stroking her and responding to her eager kisses.

He undid her belt and unbuttoned the dress down its whole length, then, quickly, he undid her bra and slid off her knickers.

She lay beneath Luke twisting and turning in an agony of frustrated passion as his loving fingers worked on her. Luke winced silently as Sally's fingers bit hard into his bare flesh as his tongue flicked her erect, firm, nipples.

Moving down her stomach, Sally screamed and arched up as Luke's tongue found its warm, moist, target

She screamed quietly again and Luke raised himself above her, lowering himself slowly into Sally's waiting dampness.

Luke didn't even try and control her unstoppable actions, simply letting his body follow hers as she thrashed about slamming her body hard against his as he slipped in and out of her.

Her frenzied thrusting lasted for many long minutes and Luke held on tightly, riding her as best he could as she continued to arch them both upwards high above the tangled bed sheets.

Luke kissed Sally tenderly as she clutched him tightly to her and felt Sally shudder along the whole length of her body as she climaxed.

Luke placed his hands on her hips and began to slow her down and gain a regular beat, until, at last, Luke felt himself coming deep within her sweating body.

When Sally felt this, she immediately began to pump again, but Luke managed to control her urges this time and they reached another climax, this time, almost together.

Luke removed his hands from her hips and began to worry her hair as he kissed Sally's lips, making love yet again, at a tenth of their original speed. Luke felt her tight uterus muscles gripping him from within and pushed even harder into her, feeling the extra sensuality as he did so as he quickened his pace again.

At last, he grinned down at her flushed face and disheveled hair.

" You okay, babe?"

" God." Lou. I've never, ever, felt as good as I do right now. My whole body seems to be alive and ultra sensitive."

" Mine too, Sall. You is one magic lady, I mean that."

" Truly?"

" Yeh. Believe me, baby. You is the best, ever."

" You're not gong off me, already, are you?"

Luke looked deeply into her eyes, and smiled as he pushed himself into her waiting body once more.

" Go off you? Never, baby, c'mere."

Deftly, Luke rolled Sally over and sat her upright, and she began to press herself tightly to him before rising and falling to bring them both on to another wonderful climax.

She bounced up and down above him then slowed as she worked herself into another bout of passion, easing herself down onto his stomach as he came onec more inside her.

Luke grinned up at Sally as she led them and closed his eyes in pure pleasure as she squeezed her muscles tightly as she slid up and down on his solid growth.

Backing off him, Sally flicked her tongue over his body as she moved downwards and he soon felt her hot lips taking him into her mouth as her lips and tongue worked on him.

Luke had to dig his fingers hard into the sheets as Sally aroused him almost beyond control and, at last, lay back gasping as she brought her lips to his.

" Was that okay, Lou?"
" Fuckin hell, baby. I am on fire."

Sally kissed and fondled Luke once more, squirming around so that his tongue could get to her as she closed her lips over his, still erect, penis, and it was almost another two hours before they lay in each others arms, kissing and cuddling, their unstoppable passions now quelled, for the time being, at least.

As Sally stroked his stomach, they both jumped as they heard the back door bell ringing continuously.

Looking at her watch, sally gasped.

" My God. It's 6.55pm, we have to open in five minutes."

Luke made her kiss him one more before letting go, then, he hurriedly dressed and lit up a smoke.

" You go and rearrange yourself, babe, I'll sort it all out."

" Oh, Lou."

" C'mon, babe. You looks okay."

" Lou. I look as if I've been shagged solid for hours."

" Yeh, well?"

" I don't want half the town knowing about it, though, do I?"

Sally scurried off and Luke combed his hair as he hurried down the stairs, opening the back door to let Sandra, the barmaid, in.

" Sorry, I must have dropped off."

" Wot about Sally?"

" Dunno, babe, perhaps she's still out?"

Sally appeared some minutes later, still flushed and wide-eyed, and Sandra looked, but didn't speak.

They moved apart and Luke opened up the back bar, letting in the waiting faithful. The bar filled up rapidly and soon the juke box was belting out. Luke turned it up louder when 'Legs' came on, crossing to see what number it was as he'd missed it before.

Sally breezed in and grimaced.

" You lot deaf in here?"
" Wot? Sorry, can't hear you. Oh, sorry, boss."

Luke grinned and pinched her bottom as she passed. Without stopping, Sally came back past him and grabbed Luke firmly between the legs, then she was gone, and Luke breathed out slowly and thankfully.

" You look a bit rough, mate?"
" Oh. Hi Dave. Yeh, it's been busy."
" Ha. Yeh, I bet. Lou, can I talk to you?"
" You is."
" Yeh. Well. I'm bein constantly phoned up by Debbie, askin me to speak to you. She's really upset."
" Look, Dave. I've already told you, forget it. Tell her, from me, to piss right off. I don't like bein made a twat of. She can still use the cottage, but not that piss head boyfriend of hers."
" Okay, mate. I won't mention it again."
" Thank fuck for that. Now, have a drink on me."
" Cheers, Lou. Fancy a game of darts?"
" Well. I'm a bit tied up at the mo. Hang on."

He crossed to Sandra and came back, lifting the flap.

Luke played Dave and Phil so as to even up the odds a little, but still beat them 2 games to 1, buying them another round anyway.

After sticking half a dozen records on the juke box, Luke slipped back behind the bar to help reduce the queue of customers that had built up.

Sally shot in, grabbed half a lemon, and disappeared once more before Luke could make any comment.

A few of Luke's old friends had started to frequent the Falcon after hearing that Luke was back working there, one of them spoke as he offered Luke a smoke.

" How long you stayin, Lou?"
" Dunno, mate. Hang on."

As 'Legs' came on, Luke turned the juke box up once more and his friends started stamping the beat out on the floor, as they used to do in their biker days.

Luke didn't see Sally come in behind him and stood, dumbfounded, as she squeezed the lemon down his back, patting him, non-too-gently, before turning the juke box down again. Throwing Luke a pitying look she rushed off back into ther front bar.

The rest of them roared as Luke pulled the flattened lemon out, hurling it at them.

Trevor grinned.

" Whoo. Some sparky landlady, Lou. That's why we don't usually come In here."

" Why?"

" She's hell on wheels when she gets goin."

" Ha. Is that right? Bet I could tame her. Sall's like putty if you handles her right. A squeeze here, another there, and you can mould her, just like that."

The others had fallen silent as Luke spoke and his grin disappeared as he saw a set of drumming fingertips on the bar next to his.

Sally eyed him severely.

" Lou. If you're that fond of telling fairy tales, may I suggest that you join a play group, as a pupil? However, if you'd like to continue working here until you're accepted there, could you, please, apply your brutish body to putting on a new barrel? Understand that, okay, can you, or shall I draw you pretty pictures of what I want you to do? OK. A barrel of bitter, please, oh little one."

Sally's face was perfectly straight as she spoke, then she wheeled away and strode off through the front bar.

The others laughed loudly at Luke's astonished look. He was completely lost for words and quickly went below to change the barrel.

They were still laughing when he returned.

" Hey, oh little one, can we have some refills here. If you can reach the pump, that is."

" I'll reach your pissin pump in a minute, mate."

" Ha. Hey, Lou, she soon fuckin well shut you up, didn't she. Hell it's worth comin down here just for that."

They all laughed loudly and Luke saw Derrick enter.

" Hi, Derr. Want a drink?"

" No thanks, Lou. Can I have a quick word, mate?"

" Sure."

" In private."

" I'm a bit pushed."

" Okay. I'll wait."

Deciding to get it over with, Luke asked Sandra to cover and followed Derrick out into the yard.

" Lou. Wot the hell is going on?"

" How?"

" Come on. Between you and our Debbie?"

" Nothin. Nothin at all. There never was."

" Well. She sure is making life difficult at home right now. Her, and that pratt, Terry."

" Look. I took her to the dance last week. This, Terry, came over and told me to lay off his bird. So I did, not that there was ever anythin between me and Debs."

" And what happened in here the other night?"

" He hit a girl, so I hit him. Next time, I'll kill the arsehole."

" That's another, different, story from his. Debbie's agrees with yours, but Terry says different."

" Look. I don't give a shit, man. Just keep them away from me."

" Both of them?"

" Yeh. Be easier that way. I don't want to do bird again for crackin that bastard, Der. But if I has to, then I will."

" Okay, Lou. I'll try and sort it all out. Cheers."

" Cheers, mate."

Luke returned to the bar to find Sandra the centre of attention as she flashed her smokes. Taking one, Luke hummed along to the tune and Mike grinned.

" Strange one for you, Lou?"

" Yeh. Well, I'll have to stick to ballads seein how I ain't allowed to stamp no more."

" Give up fightin her, mate."

" Hell. She's too fuckin old to fight. Oh, shit."

Sally appeared with a soda siphon and began to soak Luke with the contents.

" Too old, am I, you bloody worm."

Nigel grinned.

" Hey, Lou. She's getting personal now."

Sally turned the siphon on them all, emptying it finally over Luke's head.
She bounced off again and Luke looked out at the world through dripping hair.

" This place is a fuckin mad house."

Nigel laughed.

" It's cos you're here, Lou. God. Is she ever active. She just keeps poppin up from nowhere."

Billy shook his head.

" I'm fuckin well soaked. We'll all have to keep quiet now. Thanks, Lou."

Luke scowled.

" Wet? You ain't the only fucker."

Sally stood in the doorway and threw a bucket and mop at Luke.

" You'd better clean up your mess before someone slips on it. God. Look at the state of you, Lou. Oh, and mind your language, please."

She sighed heavily as she surveyed him with her hands on her hips. Then she left.

Nigel laughed again.

" She's fuckin unbelievable, Lou. You sure you ain''t been coachin her?"

" I ain't answerin that."

Luke proceeded to mop both sides of the bar, then putting the mop back in the bucket, turned to see Dave grinning at him over the bar.

" If you even fuckin well speaks, I'll hit you."

" Okay, Lou. Just fill them up, will you. You ain't out of soda, are you?"

Luke scowled but grinned in the end and saw Carol and a few of her friends trooping in and turned to serve them next.

Carol grinned.

" Hey there, stranger. Lou, you remember that Mrs Hinton that used to keep the Railway?"

" Yeh."

" She won half a million after she left, jammy cow."

" Yeh. Though she made enough out of us in the old days, bastard landlords, they wants..."

Luke stopped as Sally appeared carrying a box of crisps.

" Please, don't let me stop you, Lou. You were saying, about landlords and, presumably, landladies?"

" Aw. Nothin, babe."

Luke winked at her as she stood, straight-faced, before him.

"Something wrong with your eye, Lou? Try washing after you get up."

Luke shook his head and turned, to face them all.

" Okay, you lot. Listen. I give up. Okay. I give up."

Sally gazed around trhe bar, toeing a piece of plastic across the floor towards him.

" Looking at the state of this bar, I can see that without you telling us all."

When she had gone, Luke flashed his smokes.

" You can't bloody win, can you?"
" You, can't, you mean. We're all stayin out of this. Fill them up again, Lou, before anythin else happens."

The rest of the night passed quietly enough and, after he had bade his friends goodbye, he locked up for the night and collected the empty glasses,tipping the full ashtrays into the bin as he went.
He had finished washing up by the time that Sandra left, just as Sally came in to empty the till.

" Nearly finished, Lou?"
" Yeh. Almost. I'll give it a sweep through in a mo."
" Okay. I'll go and count up, then put the kettle on."
" Yeh, sounds good."

Luke finished off tidying up with the lights off, except for those over the bar. Stacking the stools on the tables, Luke swept the debris up that littered the floor, then, deciding to mop it, he soon had the floor shining.

He joined Sally just as she was putting the takings into the safe.

She closed it with a sigh and smiled over at Luke.

" Right. Coffee time. Check all the doors and windows for me, will you please?"

" Sure, Sall."

When Luke rejoined her, the coffee was ready and he sat next to Sally in the darkened dining room.

" Ah. I needed that. I'm shattered. Not enough exercise."

" Or, too much?"

He grinned.

" Naw. I can't really remember wot it's like."

" Oh. Thanks very much. Excuse me."

Sally gave a big yawn.

" Well. I'm ready for bed, Lou, don't know about you? Only two guests in for the morning and they both want late breakfast's, thank God."

" Yeh. Me too. Night, Sall."

Luke looked at her as he rose and crossed to the stairs.

He quickly undressed and flopped onto his bed after putting the lights off.

His door opened quietly and Sally stood framed there in a semi transparent nightie.

" Okay, Lou. I've come crawling to you, you rat, as you obviously don't want to make the first move. But in my bed, this time, it's bigger."

Luke grabbed his clothes, grinning to himself, and was soon settled beside Sally in her double bed, holding and caressing her eager and supple body in another session of pure passion.

Chapter 6

Luke soon settled into the Falcon, with Sally accepting him as her lover in private but, at Luke's suggestion, keeping it from everyone else, which was futile, as the whole town was aware of what was going on between them by dinner time the first day, as every well-kept secret in Bromyard was.

Luke decided to visit the cottage again to try and get some more songs done, and, lifting his guitar and amp from the car early one morning, carried them into the deserted cottage.

Luke soon sorted a pattern out, writing the words first and humming a tune over and over again until he felt satisfied with it.

Luke built up the background tracks by first over-dubbing the drums, then bass guitar, followed by lead guitar, and, when required, the synthesizer.

But, this was a slow process and, after several days, Luke was still far from satisfied with his efforts, but, as it was nearly opening time, he left things as they were for the following day, wishing that Debbie was present to sort his problem out for him.

However, as he had to stay and help Sally out over a very busy weekend, it was the Monday of the following week before he returned to the cottage.

He knew that someone had been there, as his papers had been disturbed, guessing that it was Debbie collecting more of her stuff, catching a faint trace of her perfume in the still air.

Luke switched on the cassette player to replay his tape but was surprised to find Debbie's voice talking to him from it.

Her clear, bright, voice stilled his hand as it moved to switch it off again.

" Lou, as this is probably the only way that I can get in touch with you, I'm going to have a go. I hope that you listen to all of this. Please, Lou, don't switch this off until the end, just make your own mind up afterwards.

I am really baffled and unhappy, Lou, as I hear so many different stories.

To go back to 'THAT' night at the dance.

I wasn't really that interested in Terry, I'm still not and never have been if the truth was known. But, like I said to you at the time, I, suppose, that I am going out with him, in that sense, in as much as he asked me out, and I had accepted.

Now, with you. You were a friend, you have never asked me out, and it was you, Lou, that wanted to keep our relationship on a purely business level, remember?

It was obvious that our kisses and dances were a bit of fun to you, nothing more, so, I accepted that, sort of, anyway. I didn't really have any choice really, did I?

So, I can't understand what all of this fuss is about. You told Dave to tell me that I'd messed you about. How have I messed you about?

You were quite horrid to me that night, Lou. I don't know why though? It really hurt me, what you said to me that night. Why won't you even see me anymore, Lou? If I was a true friend to you, why have you gone off me so quickly?

I can't see how you could have been jealous of Terry as, to you, I'm only a silly young girl that you're out for a bit of fun with?

I won't tell you what I think and feel on that side of things, just listen to Chicago, 'You're The Inspiration; , or, Air Supply ' I'm All Out Of Love' . Or, try Abba ' One Of Us'? Perhaps, then, you just might get a glimmer of what I feel. Call it a girl's silly fantasies if you like.

I really enjoyed your company, Lou , and I was content to let things stay the way that you wanted them, with the occasional kiss and dance together. It was something to look forward to, after all. Very special to me, Lou.

I thought that we could do some great songs together, still could do, in fact. I could put up with your worst faults, and with you living at the Falcon, with Sally. But, please be my friend again, Lou, that's all that I want, for now.

That's all for now. If you want to reply, please leave a tape in the machine for me to listen to.

Oh. Thanks for letting me still use the cottage, Lou. I really appreciate it, even though it takes me ages to walk out here, hint, hint.

A little song follows, which I've called 'If I Didn't Have You'. Take care, Lou, and, I miss you, I really do."

Debbie sang the song beautifully and emotionally and Luke listened to it several times before playing the rest of the songs on the tape, those that Debbie had suggested he listen to.

Luke replayed her song yet again and sat, thoughtfully smoking, as he replayed her spoken message to him.

Luke sat at the table for long minutes, then, picking up a pen, began to write.

Within ten minutes he had a song written, which he titled, 'Debbie'.

Luke put in a clean tape and pressed play.

182

" Hi Debbie. I've just been listening to your tape. It was good, babe, as everything that you do is. Your song, 'If I Didn't Have You' was magic, Debs, really it was.

Okay, as you've picked Chicago, perhaps you ought to listen to Paul Young, 'Everytime You Go Away'?

I can't tell you why I got uptight at the dance, girl, perhaps I was under a false impression about you. Was I jealous? Yeh, perhaps I was. I don't think of you as a bit of fun on the side, neither, or wotever you mean. You is right about you bein young though. I'm twice your age, nearly as old as your old man. I wander off all over the place when the fancy takes me, too, babe. So, rather than risk breaking your beautiful little heart, a casual friendship was the safest bet all round, though I never consciously thought it out like that, Debbie, babe.

I'm not goin to give you a long lecture here on things, but I guess you're better off now. Things is less complicated for you now I'm out of your life. And you certainly don't need me for songs, neither, as you can do your own perfectly, and carry me along with you.

I'll leave you with the words that I've just written. Stick a tune to it for us, babe. It's called 'Debbie', and it's written for you, and to you, baby. Take care. I think of you all the time, Debbie. And, yeh, I really does miss you, babe."

He propped the paper with the song on next to the cassette player and quickly left the cottage, afraid that he might change his mind if he stayed any longer.

It was Thursday before Luke returned to the cottage, seeing instantly that someone had been there after his last visit.

The cassette player was there with a fresh tape in and, as Luke sat down, he switched the player on.

" Hi again, Lou. Thanks for the tape. I listened to the Paul Young song and read the song that you wrote for me. It was so lovely. I did put a tune to it for you, not too badly, even though I do say so myself.

You do talk some squit sometimes, don't you, Lou? On the one hand, you say that you move on when the fancy takes you, and that you live from day to day. But, in the very next breath, you say the opposite to me. I'm not a baby, Lou. Okay, so you might be a granddad. But I'd never believe it if I didn't know differently. Anyway, what's age got to do with things? The way that you rabbit on you'd think that you never went with anyone under 30, and we all know that's not true, don't we, Lou, dear?

Just how many 'fair young maidens' have you been with, and how often have you ever given a second thought to breaking their hearts in the past? Not to mention Ruth. Oh yes, we all know about that, Lou.

184

You waffle on far too much. Personally, I think it's your brain going, your brain cells do deteorate with old age, did you know that? It's a well-proven scientific fact, actually, Lou.

Personally, I don't know, and I don't really care, Lou, one way or the other.

I'm off now. Byeee.

Oh. If you want the song 'Debbie' played, you'll have to ask me, very, nicely, in person. To do that, Turn this machine off and just turn around."

Luke sat staring at the tape player as it hissed on, then, he turned around in his seat.

Debbie stood in the doorway leaning casually on the post, her guitar in her hand.

" You didn't turn the machine off, Lou."

Pressing the button, Luke rose and slowly crossed to Debbie.

" That was a neat stunt, Debs?"

" Wasn't it just."

" I didn't know you was here."

" That was the general idea, Sir."

" Okay. I'm sorry for all the childishness. Can I hear the song?"

" I said that you'd have to ask me nicely. I'd hardly call that nice, would you?"

" Okay. Debbie, baby. Will you please play the song for me?"

" Hmm. Okay."

She moved over to the stool and crossed her legs before taking her guitar up.

Debbie sang it beautifully and strongly, dropping her voice huskily to finish.

" Okay, was it, Lou?"

" Jeez. Bloody ace, baby."

" Hmm. I can't really sing about myself. Can I change the title?"

" No way, babe. That's your song."

" Thanks, Lou. You'll have to sing it, then?"

" No way. Not after hearin you sing it. No one else could come anywhere close to you, babe."

" Oh. Thanks, again, Lou. All these compliments."

" Yeh. Well. You're worth it, Debs."

" Am I?"

" Oh, yeh."

Debbie began strumming and she soon began on the Elaine Page/ Barbara Dickson song ' I Know Him So Well'. Luke listened, enthralled, as she sang, changing the 'Him' to 'You' as she smiled over at Luke.

She finished, adding.

" I mean that, too, really I do, Lou. Now, to change the subject slightly. Do you reckon that you could do a duet on that one with me?"
" Try it, shall us, babe?"

It took them an hour and a half to perfect it, but, by then, they had something that they were reasonably happy with.

The rest of the day passed quickly, and it was soon time for Luke to get back in time for opening. Debbie stayed on at the cottage as her Dad was coming to fetch her, and Luke promised to pick her up early the next morning so that they could spend another day at the cottage. Luke treated her to a long and passionate kiss before leaving, one that Debbie responmded to to with equal, if not more, fervour.

Sally was as busy as ever as Luke entered and waved a hand at him.

" Oh, Lou. Can you change both barrels of bitter for me when you have a sec. We've just had a big party booking for 8.30pm tonight, so, I'm going to be a bit pushed.

" Yeh. No sweat, Sall, we'll cope okay."

" Had a good day?"

" Yeh, the best for some time. We actually got some work done."

" We?"

" Yeh. She's back."

" She? You didn't say?"

" You didn't ask. Anyway, that's got nothin to do with it. It's a working relationship only. She sure can knock out some good tunes though."

" Do I know her?"

" Dunno. She comes in here now and again."

" Ah. Oh well. Back to work. Only half an hour until opening time."

After putting the new barrels on, Luke put on the bar lights, stocked up the jukebox and opened the door.

Trade wasn't too brisk to start with, but by 7.15pm there were quite a few present, including some of Luke's old friends again, who laughed and joked with him whenever he was free.

Phil took up Nigel's quiet question with a grin.

" Yeh. Hey, Lou. Have you managed to tame the old dragon yet?"

" Wot?"

" Lou. C'mon mate. Old whirlwind Sally. Or is she still ridin you hard?"

Luke thought back to the previous night in bed with her. She certainly had ridden him hard then, and he grinned at them.

" Yeh. I lets her have her own way, it's easier. Saves her gettin in a major strop. Mind, underneath, she knows I'm the fuckin boss."

Right on cue, Sally appeared and all eyes turned to her, including Luke, with a sinking feeling.

Sally looked at Luke as she changed some notes in the till, then gave him a hard stare as she left.
Phil laughed.

" I reckon she's goin to give you the boot before long, Lou. You shouldn't keep runnin her down."

Luke didn't say anything, but turned to serve Dave and his friends who had just entered. Carol came in after them, trailing Debbie behind her.
They all looked at Luke, Dave was obviously not sure what to say or do, and looked very nervous as he waited for Luke's reaction to seeing Debbie there.
Luke simply grinned at them.

" Hi folks, wot's it tonight then. My round."

As Debbie came forward, Luke winked at her.

" Hi Debs, babe. Busy?"
" Not anymore, Lou. I finished off a couple of songs after you'd left."
" Brill. You still goin tomorrow?"
" Oh yes. Are you?"
" Hope so, babe. I'll pick you up about 8.30am, okay?"
" Great, Lou. I'll have the kettle on."

Dave grinned .

" You two friends again, then?"

Luke looked hard at him as he winked at Debbie.

" Yeh, just friends. Okay?"
" Sure, Lou. Sure. Thank fuckin God for that."

They all went and sat down together, and Luke returned to his cronies, laughing with them and telling them some of the places that he'd visited since leaving Bromyard back in the 1960's.

Manda and Ruth came in next, spoke to some of Luke's friends and Ruth came up to the bar, smiling softly as she spoke to Luke.

" Hi, Lou. Two halves of cider please."
" Sure. There you goes, babe. On me, okay?"
" Whoo. Cheers. Want a fag, Lou?"
" Yeh, thanks, Ruth."

She lit two up and passed one over to Luke, placing it between his lips.
Luke glanced over at Nigel as he shook his head.

" Hell, Lou. You ain't changed, have you?"
" Hey, c'mon, mate. She's a customer. Got to please them, ain't I?"

As Manda wandered over to Dave's group, Ruth stayed at the bar watching Luke as he served the other customers. Her lovely young face was alive with admiration, and was not lost on Phil and the rest, though they confined their comments to themselves, giving Luke the occasional lewd wink as they looked at him and then, Ruth.

Luke gazed at Ruth, remembering what Debbie had said earlier to him, she obviously knew about something, but Luke was unsure as to what. He leaned over the bar towards her and whispered, their heads close together.

" Ain't told no one, has you?"

" No. Course I ain't. Why. You ashamed?"

" Naw. Course I ain't, girl. But keep it cool, okay? You'll be the one that gets the shit, not me."

" Huh. I can take care of myself. But, don't worry, I'll keep it quiet for you."

" Good girl."

" Can I see you again, later?"

" Wot. Tonight?"

" Yeh."

" I'm a bit busy, babe."

" Oh. I see. Never mind then, Lou. I understand."

" Meanin?"

" That I was a one night stand, yeh?"

" C'mon, Ruth. You know that ain't true."

" Huh. You seem to be givin me the elbow now. Only wants me when I'm pissed, is that it?"

" Fuck off, baby. Don't start that shit."

" Yeh. I'll see you around then, Lou."

As she moved away, Luke reached over the bar and grabbed her arm.

" Look. I just don't want you to get too attached to me, Ruth. I may be off tomorrow and you wouldn't see me again."

" Okay. But give me a chance while you're here. Or don't you fancy me now, is that it?"

" Course I does. Look. Stick around. Yeh, comin Dave."

Luke served the waiting customers then fell in with Phil and the group, talking about the old days.

Sally came past and kicked his ankle.

" Oh. I'm sorry, Lou. I didn't see you there. You were so still, I thought that you were part of the furniture."

They all laughed as she left and Luke refilled Ruth's glass, taking another smoke off her.

He stayed chatting to Ruth for a while, coming back after he had served more customers.

Phil and the rest left, and after a lot of parting banter, Luke collected the empty glasses together and mopped the top of the bar dry with a large green cloth beermat.

Ruth moved slowly across to the juke box and stood studying the records. Luke gazed over at her, thinking how attractive and well built she was, there was certainly no doubt about that.

Ruth seemed to glide back across the floor to him, seating herself on a vacant stool with her head on one side.

" You look thoughtful, Lou?"
" Yeh. Just rememberin the other night with you."
" Oh. And you liked it?"
" And how, Ruth."

Her warm smile pleased him as he moved away to serve more customers.

Dave came over with Tony to buy another round of drinks and glanced enquiringly at Ruth.

" You joinin us or stayin over here all night?"
" Oh. I'm okay here."

Luke looked at her and nodded over to the others.

" Don't ignore your friends, baby. They're the ones that buy the drinks."

She looked at Luke and smiled.

" Yeh. Okay. I'll take the hint."

Luke wondered if she was putting it on for the benefit of the others and winked at Dave, who grinned back as he carried the refills over to their table.

Luke looked across at Debbie, she was talking to Carol and another girl and seemed to be enjoying herself. She caught his eye and picked up her drink, mouthing 'Cheers' at him. Her little smile brightening Luke up as he turned away to serve more customers.

As trade slackened off, Luke joined Dave and Tony for a game of darts, which he won. Then, as Tony sat down, Dave suggested a game of doubles, picking Carol as his partner.

Luke picked Debbie, much to Ruth's very obvious annoyance, as the game began.

This evened the game up, for Luke didn't try too hard, encouraging Debbie and showing her how to hold and throw the darts correctly.

Dave and Carol won the first game and, when Luke came back from serving more customers, they began game two.

It was the first to win 5 games, and the score stood at four-all now. Dave needed 74 and Luke, 93, and it was Debbie's shot.

She threw her first dart, scoring seven. Her second netted her seventeen and her thrird fell out onto the mat.

Dave grinned broadly.

" Cheers, Deb. 69 left for you, Lou. My shot."

Debbie clung tightly to Luke, her head buried in his shoulder, looking up as Dave threw.

" Twenty, leaves fifty four."

He threw again, scoring another twenty.

" Leave me double seventeen. Just like... that."

Dave threw the dart and it landed, dead centre, in the double seventeen.

His eyes were wide with disbelief as he threw up his arms and yelled.

" Yippee. We bloody well won, Lou."

Debbie bent her head to his chest and bit him gently through his tee shirt.

" Sorry, Lou. I lost it for you."

" Naw, babe. I was too cocky. I shouldn't have left it so long."

" Forgive me then?"

" Nothin to forgive, Debs. And don't nibble me."

" But you're tasty, Lou."

" If you likes beer-stained tee shirts, yeh."

She wrinkled up her nose and smiled at him, still holding on to Luke's arm.

" It's you that beer stained."

" Cheers."

" Only teasing, Lou."

She lifted herself up onto her toes and planted a big, smacking, kiss right on Luke's lips, her tongue seeking his out eagerly, then bent her head to his ear as she smiled sweetly at him.

" That'll give the competition something to chew on."

Then, louder, she said.

" That's for making you lose."

Then Debbie returned to her seat next to Carol. Dave started whistling as he grinned and Luke moved away to the bar to buy the winners their drinks.

Then, it started.

Apparently, Debbie had moved her handbag off the table, knocking off an ashtray, which had, presumably, landed in Ruth's lap.

The two girls were on their feet across the table, Ruth's voice raised.

" You stupid cow."

" I'm sorry. It was an accident."

" Like fuck it was, too. You've been tryin to annoy me all evening."

" I haven't."

Debbie's voice was still low and calm, but Ruth's had risen even higher, both in volume and pitch.

" Oh yes you have, you cow."

" I'm not a cow, either."

" You are. A stupid, frustrated, cow."

" I'm not frustrated, either."

" Huh. Not much you ain't."

" If anyone's frustrated, it's you, Ruth."

" Wot?

The juke box fell silent for once, and Sally stood in the front bar archway, listening, but not moving, as Debbie continued.

" You heard. You hang around people, getting them to buy you drinks, and for what?"

" What do you know about it, yeh? Look at tonight, with Lou. Hangin on to him like that, as if you belonged there."

" I do, as much as you do."

" Ha. That's all you know about it, you cow-face."

" Well. At least I don't flaunt it around like you do, you tramp."

" I'm not. You cow. At least Lou appreciates me."

" How?"

" Ask him. I doubt if he'd ever sleep with you, even if he was desperate."

" He's slept with you?"

" Find out, cow face."

" You blasted little tramp. You slag."

Sally had moved forward with her usual speed, and now stood between the two girls, holding Ruth back.

" Come on girls, cool it please, or you'll have to leave."

" She called me a slag."

" Perhaps she's right."

" Wot. You fuckin old bitch."

Ruth went for Sally, but was stopped dead by a ringing blow to her cheek from Sally's open- handed slap.

" Now. Get out, please, before I forget that I'm a lady."

Ruth, red faced and livid, stormed sullenly out of the bar without looking at anyone, her eyes fuming and jaw set solidly as she slammed the door loudly behind her.

Sally came back behind the bar and cast Luke a quick look as she passed him.

" The things one hears in pubs, eh, Lou?"

Debbie had sat back down and now glared at Luke, who busied himself with serving once more, calling Dave over to take his order.
He grinned as he picked up the tray.

" Whoops, Lou?"
" Yeh, fuckin major, whoops, too."

Luke crossed to the juke box, selected Chicago ' It's Hard To Say I'm Sorry' then went over to Debbie and whispered in her ear.

" Listen to the words, Deb, it's for you."

Going back behind the bar, Luke turned the volume up and watched as Debbie listened, but didn't look at him.

When the record was over, Debbie rose and selected her own record after some hesitation, then sat down omce more.

Dave came over, grinning.

" Deb says this is for you. Getting interesting, ain't it?"

Luke listened as Brian Adams 'Run To You' started up, not quite able to work out how he was meant to take it?

Luke's next choice was ' Every Time You Go Away', which was followed by Debbies, ' All Out Of Love'.

As she sat down again, they all pointed at Luke, chorusing.

" It's for yoo-hoo."

Luke's next choice was ' I Should Have Known Better', which the group chorused to her, then swung back to Luke as Debbie's next choice started, ' I Just Called To Say I Love You'.

Luke's final choice was REO Speedwagon ' I Can't Fight This Feeling' and Debbie's was, ' You're The Inspiration' after which, the whole group clapped.

Dave stood up and laughed.

" I declare this conest a draw."

There were more loud cheers and whistles, and Luke refilled their glasses for them.
Debbie sat, looking unsure of what to do, and Luke beckoned her over to the bar.
She came slowly, looking apprehensive, standing before him with her hands resting lightly upon the bar top.

" Debs, for your sake, I want to keep this pretty casual."
" Keep, what, casual?"
" Our friendship."
" That's okay. I understand. After all, this is only a bit of fun, isn't it?"
" Yeh. Sure. As long as you realise that?"

" Of course I do. Did you sleep with Ruth, or not, Lou?"

" Wot?"

"Are you deaf, Lou?"

"Babe. I...."

"Oh, never mind. It's pretty obvious that you did sleep with her, isn't it?. Can I go back to my seat now?"

" Oh, sure."

Luke's eyes watched Debbie as she walked slowly back to her seat. He would have given a lot of money to be able to read her thoughts right then.

Dave came back in from the toilet and motioned Luke over, whispering in his ear.

" Ruth's outside, she wants to see you, mate."

" Shit. I can't get out now."

" She'll still be there when you close, don't worry."

After the bar was emptied and closed, Luke set about washing the glasses and tidying up. It was gone midnight when he went outside and found that Ruth was, indeed, still waiting for him.

Wordlessly, he led her to his car and drove out to the countryside.

As they stopped, Ruth turned to him, her eyes holding his in the gloom.

" Well. Why didn't you stick up for me?"

" You was doin okay on your own. Anyway, I thought we was goin to keep this quiet?"

" I'm sorry, Lou. It just slipped out. I had to say something to stop her. Are you really goin out with Debbie?"

" Naw."

" Have you ever?"

" Nope."

" Never screwed her?"

" Never."

" Well. Well. I bet I did shock her, then?"

" You shocked the whole fuckin bar, too."

" Shit to them, Lou."

They were soon in each other's arms and making love long into the early hours of the morning, and when Luke finally returned to the Falcon, he went straight to his own bed, falling asleep on top of the sheets, still fully clothed.

By 8.30am, Luke was at Debbie's and found her waiting at the gate for him, flopping into the seat beside him as they took off.

" Mum says come to tea."

" I can't babe, can I. I have to open up?"

" Not until 6.00pm. We're having tea at around 4.00pm, so, that solves that little problem. Doesn't it, Lou, dear?"

" Yeh. I guess. Schemer."

" It was Mum's idea, actually."

" Yeh, after some persuading, I bet?"

" I didn't have to use much really. I was quite disappointed."

The day went very well for them, and they ran through several songs, listening to their results on the cassette player.

Around 1.00pm, several cars pulled up and Dave and the gang spilled into the cottage, grinning widely.

" Dah-Rah. We're here."

Debbie grinned at him.

" Oh, yes. Lou, dear. I asked them to pop over to listen. Don't mind, do you?"

" Naw. No probs, babe."

They played through a selection of numbers, including ' I Know Him/Her So Well' and finished to loud and appreciative applause.

" That's brill, you two, honestly."

Carol was only one who congratulated them and, as they all swept out, Luke told them to call again whenever they liked.

Left alone again, they came together in a deep passionate embrace before sorting out more tunes, leaving soon after so as to arrive at Debbie's at a little after 4.10pm.

Mo grinned.

" Hi, you two. Nearly on time. Grub's up in 5 minutes. Had a good day?"

" Fab, thanks, Mum. Carol and the mob came. They seemed to like us, too."

" I should think so too, dear. You'll have to put on a show soon."

" Hmm. We'll see. I don't think that Lou will be too keen on that, Mum."

Mo grinned as she winked at Luke.

"Oh, I'm sure that he will, love. Lou is a great showman, aren't you, Lou?"

" Nah, Mo, I was allus the quiet one. You lot was too busy hoggin the limelight to notice me."

"Haha, very funny, Lou. They could write a book about your escapades."

"Yeh? No fucker would buy it, though, Mo."

Debbie grinned over at Luke.

"I would. I reckon it would be fascinating. A true window on the world, a historical reference on life as it was. A peek inside the mind of one of lifes true gentleman."

"You finished, girl?"

"Yes, thanks, Lou."

Mo was laughing now, and coughed.

"Well, Lou, that's a good descrition of you. Haha, a true gentleman, just as I remember you, Lou."

Lou had to excuse himself eventually, and, after pecking Mother and Daughter lightly on their cheeks, arrived at the Falcon with only 15 minutes to spare, where he set about checking the barrels.

Sally was busy in the dining room, making sure that all was ready.

" I think that's all now, Lou. Is the back bar ready?"

" Yup. All ready to roll."

" What happened to you last night, or shouldn't I ask?"

" It was pretty late when I got in. Didn't think you'd appreciate my tender devotion at that time?"

" I didn't even hear you come in. I left the door open for you."

" Yeh, sorry."

Luke kissed her tenderly and long in the darkened bar and Sally flew eagerly into his arms, returning his embraces with fierce passion.

The night passed quickly for Luke, as did the following few days.

Their friends came around the cottage the following weekend, plus several more of their friends, too. All said that they sounded great and Luke and Debbie worked with ever more effort at perfecting their act.

They visited the cottage most days and, the following Friday, Debbie asked Luke to take her to another dance, this time with a DJ and a group who were playing at Saltmarsh.

The group were called Bandy and were supposed to be quite good.

Sally didn't object to Luke taking the evening off, and he rolled up to pick Debbie up at 7.15pm before they stopped off at the Falcon to meet up with the others.

She wasn't quite ready when he called, so he sat drinking coffee as he waited for her.

Mo came over and kissed Luke long and fully, withdrawing with a little smile at his expression.

" Hmm. Come again, soon."

Luke was interrupted in mid sentence as he chatted to Mo by the arrival of Debbie at the door. She wore a deep red-coloured dress with little yellow flowers decorating the sleeves and bodice. A golden chain hung loosely around her slim waist and her beautiful hair shone magically as she moved forward into the room, the lights catching and reflecting the golden combs that she wore on each side of her head.

" Jesus fuckin Christ. Debs, you looks so bloody beautiful, babe."

She smiled warmly with obvious growing delight.

" Do you really think so?"
" I knows so, babe. Whoo. You is tasty."

Mo laughed.

" I think that he's finally noticed you, love. So, it was worth it."

" Mum. I just threw this on."

Luke laughed.

" Baby. Wot can I say, except, wow."

Luke whistled at her as they walked to the car and held the door open as she slid elegantly into the passenger seat.

Turning to her, he shook his head.

" You is a knockout, baby."

" Okay, Lou. Don't overdo it, we're only friends, remember? Hmm. I do feel nice tonight, though."

" Don't you always?"

" Okay. I feel extra nice tonight."

As they stood outside the Falcon car in the car park, Debbie came eagerly into Luke's arms, kissing him passionaly and long.

Luke sighed as he smiled down at her.

"Baby, you is absolutely beautiful."

Dave and the gang did a double-take when Debbie followed Luke into the Falcon and Luke grinned.

" Meet my friend."

He stood next to her in his old Levi's and tee shirt and Debbie sniffed.

" Bit of a tatty old so-and-so, aren't you, Lou?"
" Sor-ry."
" Still. You car's nice, that's the main thing."

They all laughed at this and Luke paid for the round as Dave grinned.

" You scruffy git."

Debbie cut in.

" Hey. He's my minder, aren't you, Lou?"
" Yeh."

He squared up to Dave, cuffing him lightly around the ear.

" Watch wot you say to my princess, or I'll have you, boy."

Again, the whole crowd erupted into laughter at Luke's expression and they all stood chatting as they sipped their drinks.

As sally breezed through the bar, Luke introduced her to Debbie.
She was impressed, Luke could see that from the look in Sally's eyes.

" So, you're Lou's singing partner? I've heard so much about you Debbie, and, I like your songs a lot."
" Thanks very much."
" You'll have to come here and perform for me sometime."
" That would be nice, thanks."

Debbie crossed to the juke box and Luke gazed after her.
Sally passed him a smoke.

" Just good friends Lou?"
" Yeh, s'right, babe."
" Who's suggestion was that?"
" Mine, Sall, all mine."
" Oh. I see."

" Yeh. Shot you right up the arse, didn't it?"
" Pardon?"
" Well. Fishin, like that."
" Sorry, I'm sure."

She laughed as she moved away.

" Anyway, have a nice time, and I'll see you later,
okay, possibly?"
" Yeh. I'll be there, baby."
" Good. You'd better be."

Debbie came back, humming quietly to the tune and
scanned the drinks on the counter.

" Is this one mine?"
" Yeh. You did want cider?"
" Oh, yes please. Hmm. It's nice and bubbly. I like a
bit of fizz."
" You'd make it fizzy if it was flat, babe."
" Oh, Lou. Come on. Mum's not around anymore,
you don't have to pretend, you fool."

Luke merely shrugged as he lit up another smoke,
tossing the packet over to Dave and the crew.
They all left together in a five car convoy, Luke giving
four of them a lift in the XJS.

Dave tried to burn Luke off in his Mini Cooper, but Luke pulled easily away from him on the straight, thundering up the hills at over 100mph.

They all piled into the dancehall together, Luke paying for them all, and they set about filling up the bar.

The DJ was the one from the previous dances and he waved at Luke, who held up an empty glass. The DJ nodded and Luke took the pint over to him, setting it on the edge of the stage.

" Cheers, Lou. I'm Trev, by the way. I must say, your Deb is looking extremely lovely tonight."

" Yeh. Ain't she just. I can see I'll have to watch you."

" Don't worry. I know that you two are closely attached, so I'll leave well alone."

Debbie grinned impishly at his side.

" Oh. Lou and I are only good friends. We have a working partnership, nothing more."

" Oh, yeh? Is that true, Lou?"

" Yeh. I guess so, we're just mates."

" What do you do, together?"

" We write and play songs."

" Oh. I'll have to listen to you sometimes. Deb, give you some tips, like."

Since learning that Luke and Debbie were not an item, Trev's interest had immediately grown in Debbie, and he smiled warmly at her.

" You look very beautiful tonight, Debbie, as you always do, of course."
" Oh. Thanks."

Trev moved towards her and they were soon laughing and joking, making Luke feel more than a little put out for some reason as he watched them and moved thoughtfully away with his glass.

He watched as the group gave their kit a final check over as Trev's disco boomed out and, when he glanced at Debbie again, saw that Trev had his hand on her arm and she was smiling sweetly at him.

Then, across the floor, he saw Manda, Ruth and company and, putting his glass down, moved over to join them.

Ruth smiled warmly at him.

" Hi Lou."
" Hi, People. Didn't see you lot arrive?"
" We were sat down over in the corner."

" On your own, Lou?"

" Well. I came with Dave and Debs and that lot, but she seems busy now."

" Yeh. So I see."

Ruth danced up to Luke, stopping before him, her eyes bright.

" Never mind, Lou. Stay with us idiots, we'll look after you, if you can stand it."

" Ha. I can stand anythin from you, baby."

Luke noticed Trev cross to his equipment, then, as the band started, saw him hurry back to Debbie's side as she waited for him.

" Forget her, Lou, she's enjoyin herself."

Ruth gazed up at him and Luke grinned.

" Yeh. You're right, Ruth."

Soon, they were all out on the floor as the group got under way. Debbie was, predictably, dancing with Trev and didn't even glance in his direction.

Bandy were a pretty good group who had their act tight and together and went down quite well with the

216

crowd. When they did a ballad, Luke saw Debbie move into Trev's arms and rest her head on his shoulder.

Ruth tugged at him.

" Lou. I'm here, not over there."

Luke grabbed her and they embraced as they danced, their friends looking on wonderingly as they danced and kissed openly on the dancefloor.

Luke looked up to see Debbie's eyes upon him over Trev's shoulder and, seeing his gaze, deliberately bent his head down to hers, allowing Trev him to kiss her cheek.
Luke straightened up and made for the bar, dragging Ruth with him.

" Calm down, Lou, will you?"
" I'm okay."
" No, you're not. You're as mad as a love-sick bull. You ain't going to start anything with Trev, are you?"
" No. Course I ain't."
" Good. Forget her, Lou. I told you."
" Nothin to forget, girl."
" Huh. It doesn't bloody-well look like it, either. Screwin her as well, are you?"
" No. I fuckin well ain't."
" Okay. Okay. Don't get excited."

" Well. Keep it buttoned then, okay, girl?"

" Hey. Hang on, Lou. Don't fuckin well take it out on me, just cos little miss cow-face is ignorin you. I don't have to put up with this shit off you, remember that."

" Well. You knows wot you can fuckin-well do then, don't you, girl?"

" Balls to you then. If you want her that bad, you're welcome to her, if you can get her, that is. If you want me in future, you'd better come crawlin, you fuckin arsehole."

With that, Ruth stamped off across the dancefloor and Luke banged his fist hard against the bar top with a resounding thud.

Debbie was still in Trev's arms as they danced, only breaking when the both came into the bar area.

Trev was very genial.

" Good dance, Lou?"
" It's a piss hole."
" Hey, mate. Let me buy you a drink."

He took Luke's order, handing him a full pint.

Debbie sipped her cider as Trev's arm slipped easily around her shoulders and she eyed Luke as he lt up a cigarette savagely.

" Are you okay, Lou?"

" Yeh. Fuckin brilliant. Never better, girl"

" Well, you don't look it."

" Oh. You a fuckin doctor now, is you? Fuck you and this place, I'm off."

Luke drank down his pint quickly, threw the empty glass at the bar and stormed off through the crowd.

He screamed out of the car park and drove the Jaguar like a bullet towards Bromyard, slewing to a stop in the Bay Horse car park.

After ordering his pint from the hatch, Luke carried it into one of the back rooms, gazing around at the occupants as he sat on one of the benches.

Luke nodded in greeting to a few and lit up another smoke as he gazed absently out of the darkened window.

" Got a light, Lou, please?"

" Sure."

He held up his lighter without looking, then returned it to his pocket as he took up his drink.

Luke stretched out on the bench as he gazed over at the dartboard as a game started.

" Fancy a game, Lou?"

" Yeh, fuck it, why not."

" We ain't very good, though."

" Naw. Neither is I right now, mate."

" Shall we make it three a side?"

" Suits me."

Luke's partners were Toby and Bett, and they played, Colin, Sarah and Sue.

Colin was first away, with Luke second and, as the game progressed, Luke's side steadily overtook and won the match.

Three games later they changed one of their partners, Luke getting Sue in place of Toby. The two girls together were not very good and they did it to give Colin a better chance of winning.

It worked. For they won the next two games. Luke couldn't get it together and lost the next game also.

" Okay, folks. I'll get the round is as I lost."

" Yippee."

When they all had refills, Luke joined them at their table. He thought that none were over 18 and had his doubts if a couple were even 16.

" You back for good, then, Lou?"

" Dunno, Toby. I'll see how things goes."

" My Uncle used to know you in the old days, he's told us all about you."

" Wot's his name, mate?"

" Chris Davis."

" Oh, yeh. I remembers Chris. Is he still around here?"

" Yeh. Well, he's inside right now."

" How much bird's he doin?"

" Only two years, for robbery."

" Stupid sod. Where is he?"

" Shepton Mallet. Know it?"

" Yeh. Too bloody well."

Sue was looking at Luke's tattoos and gazed at him with wide, admiring, eyes.

" Were you really a hells angel, Lou?"

" Suppose so, babe. Still is, I guess."

" Honestly?"

" Yeh. You never leaves it, really. It's a way of life, a state of mind, you know."

" Tell us about it, Lou."

" Naw. You wouldn't be interested in all that shit, baby."

" Please, Lou. Please."

Sue was totally gone on him, Luke could see that, and, she was one of those that he thought was also under 16.

" Hell. Where does I start. How old is you, anyway, babe?"

" Sixteen."

" Straight?"

" Yes. Honestly, I was three weeks ago, actually."

Toby grinned.

" Yeh, she is, Lou, honest."

" Well, I'd better get you a late birthday drink, then, hadn't I?"

Luke refilled all of their glasses and regained his seat, seeing that Sue had moved over one seat and was now right, tight, next to him.

Toby and Bett entwined, as did Colin and Sarah, and Luke grinned at Sue, offering round his smokes.

" You the odd one out, babe?"

" I hope not, Lou, yeh?"

Handing out the smokes, he grinned as he let her keep the packet and began to tell them of the old days, both in Bromyard and Worcester when he was with the Chapter.

He answered all of their questions, telling them what they wanted to know, only stopping to refill all of their glasses again.

By closing time, his 5 companions were pretty well drunk, but they all still had another for the road.

As Sue stood up, Luke noticed that she was quite a small girl, both in height and body and grinned as she weaved towards the door.

He stood chatting to them for a while before turning to Sue to watch as she tottered up the street behind the others.

Sitting in the XJS, Luke finished off his smoke before gunning the machine out into Little Hereford Street and into Pump Street. He thundered left up the High Street and drew up outside the chip shop.

Toby waved as Luke climbed out.

" Hey, Lou. Is that your motor?"
" Yeh."
" Fuckin hell, a fuckin Jag."

Luke joined them.

" I'm getting some grub. Come on, I'll get you lot some, too."
" Hey, Lou, cheers mate."

When they were all outside once more, Luke sat back inside the car, leaning his arm out of the opened window as he chatted to Toby as he tried to ignore Sue's cow-eyed glances at him.

Toby shook his head.

" Fuckin hell, Lou. I bet this car really shifts, don't it?"

" Yeh. Goes like a fuckin bomb."

" Can we have a ride, Lou?"

" Yeh. Why not. C'mon, you lot, pile in."

As the four others slipped into the back seat, Sue shot straight into the front passenger seat beside Luke and smiled warmly at him.

" Coo. This feels brill. Don't mind me bein here, do you?"

" Naw, babe. Though I'd prefer it if you was a bit closer."

She laughed at Luke and began to blush as she chewed her bottom lip and Luke fired the machine off, reversing into the Tenbury road before shooting off down the back street.

Luke raced up the Worcester road past the old tile works and hospital and, reaching the top of the Downs, turned left onto the top road and slowed, finally pulling onto the grass and coasting to a stop beneath Warren Wood.

" Chip time, folks."

They all began to eat and chat, Sue feeding several of her chips to Luke and, when they had finished, all lit up smokes and relaxed as the talk moved between many topics.

Toby exhaled and spoke, his arm out of the rear window, watching his cigarette smoke rise lazily in the still air.

" How fast did we go up here, Lou?"

" Ton and ten."

" Fuckin hell. Really?"

" Yeh."

" Hell. That's the fastest I've ever been. Hey, Lou, these fuckin seats is comfy, ain't they?"

" Yeh. Just watch wot you're doin in them, that's all."

" Haha. We will."

As Sue fiddled with the cassette player, Luke put the light on for her. She smiled sweetly at him, selected a tape and lay back with her feet up on the dash.

" Don't mind, do you, Lou?"
" Naw. I can see more of your legs like that."

Luke definitely didn't mind, as her short skirt was well above her knees and, as he spoke, she bent her legs more, allowing it to ride up almost to the tops of her legs.

Luke shook his head, a wide grin on his face as he lit up two smokes and passed one to her, and Sue gripped his hand as she took it.

" Thanks, Lou."

He released himself and leaned back in his seat with his eyes closed, his thoughts centring on Sue. Yes, she was most certainly leading him on, no doubt about that.

As Luke listened to Air Supply, he heard deep sighs coming from the back seat and grinned to himself, remembering his own youth.

Sue was watching him in the darkness and, after stubbing out her smoke, she lay back, her eyes still firmly fixed on Luke's face.

Luke turned over the tape as it drew to a close, one of his hands resting gently on Sue's leg, then he lay back once more as the other side started.

Turning his head to meet her eyes, Luke put out a hand to Sue, who took it readily, squeezing it between both of hers.

Luke pulled Sue over to him and she settled gently against his chest, her eyes wide and mouth half open.

" You okay, Sue?"

" Yeh. Thanks, Lou."

"Girl, look, you is only 16, so, take it easy, okay?"

"Lou, it's my choice to be here, I ain't no kid, really."

He kissed her waiting lips tenderly, feeling her swallowing rapidly in her nervousness, Sue didn't seem to know what to do with her hands and she kept moving them around, opening and closing them. Luke kissed them, each in turn, placing them around his neck.

Kissing her again, Sue sighed lightly as she locked her arms tightly around Luke's neck and, with a hand behind her head, his lips sought her neck, then ear as he flicked his tongue lightly over them.

Her breathing quickened as Luke explored her, running his hands lightly down her back as she tensed.

Resting his hands upon her hips, he massaging them gently.

227

As Sue's lips met his once more, Luke moved one hand down her leg in a slow, stroking, motion.

A tittering from the back seat made him stop, causing Sue to sit bolt upright.

Sarah chuckled.

" I'm sorry you lot. But if I don't have a pee quick, I'll bust."

As they let her out, Luke grinned.

" Anyone else want to go, before we gets back down to it?"

As Sarah regained her seat, no one answered and Luke turned to see them all hard at it once more, Betts skirt already up around her waist as Toby's hands got to work between her parted legs.

Luke bumped himself over to the passenger seat, Sue now on his knee, and grinned at her enquiring look.

" More room over here, babe."

He reclined the seat a few inches.

" Ah. That's better, no friggin steerin wheel now. Baby, is you sure that you wants to continue?"

Her eyes were almost imploring his as she replied, a deep sigh escaping her lips as he locked her hands behind his neck.

"Lou, please, for God's sake, I ain't a kid."

Sue restarted the tape, then leaned back against him, her lips brushing Luke's cheek as her eyes burned into his, relocking her arms tightly around his neck.

She brought her lips to his and they clung lovingly together once more as Sue increased her grip around his neck.

Soon, his hand was up her skirt and gently pushing her soft pubic hair aside as his fingers probed and stroked her. As he worked her, Sue kissed him fiercely, her tongue hotly seeking his.

Without prompting, Sue straddled her knees either side of Luke as he undid his zip and eased her knickers aside.

Positioning his aching tool, Luke worked on Sue, feeling himself sliding into her waiting wetness as she moved over him.

She was soon squirming as she felt Luke's full length sliding tightly into her.

With a last thrust, Luke pushed himself right into her and felt Sue nibbling his ear, her voice a mere whisper.

" Oh. Oh God. Lou, it's the first time for me."

" You're kiddin, girl?"

"No. I've never gone all the way before. You're the very first. I've led them on before, and let them use their fingers, but always stopped."

" Why didn't you this time, then?"

" I don't know. Oh, Lou, it's great. I just want, you."

She kissed him long and passionately, and Luke responded, moving her along with his hands as he pumped inside her in deep, long, strokes.

Luke took it easy, feeling himself filling her to the limit as he moved, and backed out a little, but Sue pushed herself back onto him firmly with a grin, and soon the car was rocking as Luke slammed her up and down above him. As Luke climaxed deep within her, Sue gave a loud scream and gasped several times in quick succession. Still at the height of his passion, Luke lifted Sue up and turned her around to face forward, guiding his solid tool back into her yearning body as he brought his lips to her ear.

" You'll like this, too, baby. Believe me."

She did, and was soon gasping once more as she kept beat with him until Luke had reached, yet another, climax.

The others had watched Luke and were now trying out the same technique and Luke looked around to see Bett's sweating face almost touching his as Toby pumped hard nto her from behind.

" God. Lou. Know any more ways?"

" Yeh, babe, fuckin loads."

For the next two hours Luke instructed them in the various ways of love making, causing Sue to almost explode with passion when his tongue began to work between her legs.

Soon, once again, the whole car was rocking as the six bodies within it became ever more frenzied in their love making.

Sue simply collapsed against Luke as they smoked quietly afterwards and he kissed her lips tenderly.

" Like it?"

" God, Lou. I thought I was going to take off. Oh God. It is such a wonderful feeling."

" Sure is, baby."

" Lou. I've never done a blow job, either. I'd really like to try though with you, please."

" Be my guest, Sue. Here, kneel on the floor in front of me."

Luke showed her, seeing the others watching also as he instructed Sue and, soon, all three girls had the three males in deep raptures of passion as their mouths and tongues worked on them.

Luke almost choked poor Sue as he shot into her mouth with such force that she gagged for several long seconds. Luke leaned back in total contentment as her lips continued to suck him into her after she had recovered.

He pulled her up onto his lap and kissed her long and hard, his tongue seeking her hungrily.
Sue responded in kind and was soon almost crying with desperate passion as their bodies twisted together.
Luke felt her hands on his, still solid, tool and sighed as he felt himself being pushed back inside her lovely body. She rose and fell above him, never faltering, save for once when she began to race away, but soon slowed down with Luke's guiding hands upon her hips.
Toby laughed as they were all smoking again.

" Fuckin hell, Lou. I'll sleep for a week after all this. How do you keep goin?"
" Practise, mate. Plenty of it."

Sue turned, wriggling herself round to face him and kissed him hungrily once more, her breath hot on his cheek.

" Lou. Oh, Lou."
" Shh, baby. You is great, you know that?"
" Am I, really?"
" Yeh. The best, angel."

He sought her lips once more and they embraced for long minutes as they lay, locked together in the nights darkness.

" See wot you been missin,babe?"
" Yeh, but I've been savin it for someone special, namely you."
" Oh Yeh, I bet."
" You wait and see, then, Lou. I'll never go with anyone else, I promise you that."

Luke didn't answer, remembering back to his own youthful promises all those years ago, none of which were ever kept once the heat of passion had subsided and reality clouded back in once more.

It was 4.25am before Luke finally hit the sack, and, again, he went to sleep fully clothed.

Sally stood grinning in the doorway, a steaming mug of coffee in one hand.

" Come on, you lazy cretin. Get up. I suppose that you were out sharing your body again, were you?"

Luke sat up groggily and grinned.

" Naw, who, me?"
" Huh. It's almost 9.00am, you dirty little stop out."
" Huh. I was talking."
" What to?"
" Who, not, wot."
" Did it purr?"
" Wot?"
" Oh. Wake up. Come on, have a wash and shave, then breakfast will be ready."
" No kiss?"
" Who from?"
" You, of course."
" I don't know, Lou. Just how many of us have you got on the go at present?"
" Only you, why."

She kissed him lightly, then rose with a wry smile.

" I do like your perfume, anyway, Lou. It suits you."

234

Luke recalled Sue's scent, finding that his clothes still smelt strongly of it. Well, that part hadn't been a dream, anyway. Luke could still actually also smell and taste Sue as he breathed in, and closed his eyes as his mind flicked back to her eager, yearning, body.

Sally looked at him and grinned, breaking his reverie.

" And, it isn't Debbie's, either?"

" You an expert on perfume, now?"

" No. But I can tell the difference, Debbie would never wear something as cheap and cheerful as that."

" Go and get me breakfast, woman."

Laughing, Sally closed the door quietly behind her and Luke rose after lighting up a smoke.

Luke felt a lot better when he came down, and even more so once he had eaten.

He pulled Sally onto his lap and kissed her warmly.

" Sall. Wotever else, you're the best."

" Oh, well. That's okay then, isn't it. I mean, to be top of the tree can't be all that bad. Lou, you weren't really out with anyone, were you?"

" Don't you trust me?"

" Frankly, no."

Thankfully for Luke, the post arrived just then, and Sally rose to sort through it, taking the pile of mail into her office as she winked happily at Luke.

Luke opened up the back bar at 10.00am, switching everything on as he went.

The juke box sprang into life from the previous night and Luke hummed along with the tunes.

Trade was quiet for a while, then Dave walked in, his face serious.

" Lou. Where the hell have you been?"

" Here, why?"

" I was looking for you all last night."

" Why?"

" Bloody, Deb. That's why. She made me drive her here, there and everywhere, looking for you."

" More fool you then, mate."

" Huh. It's okay for you. She was goin fuckin well spare at us."

" She didn't look very spare when I left her, attached to Trev. She was all over the twat."

" Well. She flew at me. Wanted to know where you had gone and who with. And, she thumped Ruth."

" Never?"

" Yeh. Smack in the kisser. Sent her flyin, arse over tit. Magic, it was, to watch. Ruth was givin her some lip, so Debs clocked her with her fuckin handbag. I thought she was goin to smack me, too."

" Why didn't she get Trev to run her around, then?"

" He wanted to, but had to do the records. He hung round her for ages afterwards, like a fuckin leech he was, but she made me go and look for you. She sat in my car and wouldn't budge. She threatened to rip it apart, so I had to take her."

" But you didn't find me?"

" Yeh. And don't I know it, too. It's a wonder she didn't wake the whole fuckin town up."

" Never mind."

" Never mind, he says. Even that Trev couldn't calm her. He tried later, even tried to take her home, but she wouldn't get out of my car. In the end, I took her home, but had to drive off again as she blew my bloody horn non stop."

" Then wot happened?"

" I stopped in town to get some cigs from the machine outside the dairy, when I came back, she'd gone."

" Gone?"

" Yeh. She must have decided to hoof it home, after all."

" Jeez. Friggin women."

" You're telling me, Lou. I've never seen Deb act like that before, real wild, she was. Ha. I bet Ruth's got a sore head this morning, too."

Luke grinned over at Dave.

" Drink?"
" Oh, yeh. Cheers, mate."

Sally shot her head around the bar door.

" Lou. Telephone call for you, dearie. From a young lady, well, she sounded young, very young in fact, called Sue?"
" Sue?"
" That's who she said. Don't tell me that you don't know anyone called Sue? Or didn't you get around to finding out her name yet?"

Luke gave Dave an exasperated look as he went through to the front bar and picked up the receiver.

" Yeh?"
" Lou. It's me, Sue, remember?"
" Yeh, course I does. Hi, babe."
" Hi. Sorry to ring, but is my handbag in your car?"

" Dunno, babe."

" It must be. Can you have a look, please?"

" Yeh, okay, girl. Hang on."

Luke ran to the car, spotted it and returned to the phone.

" Yeh. It's there."

" Oh. Thank God for that. You busy?"

" So, So. I'm at work, babe."

" Can you bring it to me?"

" Now?"

" Can you?"

" Yeh. Okay. We ain't that rushed. Where shall I meet you?"

" At the top of the Green lane, by the Bredenbury turning, okay?"

" Yeh. Be there in about ten minutes. Okay?"

" Brill. See you then, Lou."

" Yeh. Bye, babe."

Excusing himself from Sally and her curious gaze, Luke drove along the Leominster road and turned off into the long, sweeping, Green Lane. It wasn't long before he caught sight of Sue hurrying towards him as he parked on the grass verge. She still wore a miniscule skirt, though a different one from the previous night. She

239

flopped down breathlessly into the passenger seat beside Luke, closing the car door gently behind her.

" Phew."

Sue reached over and kissed Luke lovingly on the lips, then sank back onto the seat.

"Oh, God. That's better. I needed that. Ah. My bag. You know, Lou, I completely forgot about that last night, what with everything else that was going on."
" Oh yeh?"
" Uhu."
" You rushin off anywhere yet?"
" No. Why?"
" Just wondered, babe."
" This time of day?"
" Oh yeh. Anytime's good."
" Yeh. You're right, Lou. Find us a nice secluded spot somewhere, please."

When they had parked, Sue reclined her seat and they came together as she giggled, struggling out of her underwear.

Luke slipped out of his jeans as Sue pulled off his tee shirt.

Naked together, Luke began a long, slow, exploration of Sue's eager body. Her responses were forceful and demanding and, as Luke flicked his tongue down over her stomach, she arched up to him hungrily.

With Sue beneath him on the seat, Luke gently lowered himself down onto her and closed his eyes with sheer pleasure as he felt himself entering her receptive body once more.

He sought her lips, kissing her tenderly and long, lingering for many minutes as they pecked and half-kissed each other before embracing hotly again.

Sue gripped Luke with her legs tightly, pulling him down hard onto her with her arms.

" Oh God. This is so good, Lou."

Her short, panting, breath reached up to him as they clung together and he nibbled her ear gently.

" Oh. Oh. Lou. You send me berserk. I just can't control myself when I feel you inside me. Oh God."

She pulled him even harder to her and twisted her head so as to kiss him passionately and Luke held onto Sue as he sank deeply into her at each thrust of their bodies.

Climaxing, Luke carried on, repeating the process once again some minutes later as Sue arched beneath him and screamed as, she too, reached the height of her own passion.

Sue's body moved easily and she wriggled and squirmed beneath his as she felt Luke shoot his hot stickiness deep within her yet again.

" Oh. Can I go on top, Lou?"
" You bet, baby."

As they changed around, Sue knelt on the floor where Luke had been and gazed at him, stroking his erect tool with her fingers.

" Well. Second time around for me. See if I can do better than last night. Here goes."

Her hot breath aroused Luke even further and, as her warm lips closed over his shaft, he gasped with pleasure as her tongue flicked his tip and her fingers eased his foreskin back.

Luke could not control himself at all and he soon felt her darting tongue licking up his love juices as it shot into her eager mouth.

He arched up to her, sinking slowly back as his passion eased, sighing deeply.

" Fuckin hell, baby. That was some job. Jeez, I am totally fuckin gone."

Smiling, Sue raised herself up and backed onto Luke as she lowered her head forward onto the dash board, her fingers guiding him into her waitinmg wetness.

He held her around the middle and pulled her back tight up against him, letting Sue ram herself back and forth above him.

They were soon sweating and gasping in unison as Sue used her body to bring Luke to, yet more, mind blowing climaxes.

Eventually, they dressed, both reluctant to do so, but knowing that if they didn't do it then, they would be there all day.

Sue clung to Luke tightly as they sat and smoked. She was nestled comfortably on his lap and kissed him lovingly.

" I never, ever, want to let you go, Lou, believe me."

" You'll soon forget me, baby."

" I won't. I never will. I know that you'll be gone soon and that I can't stop you. But I intend to enjoy myself with you while I can."

" Okay, babe. Fair enough. But I ain't gone yet, and when I does go, I'll come back to see you."

" I'll pray that you do. I could easily spend the rest of my life with you, Lou."

They smoked on and stayed, embracing and chatting for almost another two hours as the tapes played softly.

At last, passion overtook them again and Luke pulled Sue to him, his jeans already undone by her deft fingers.

When he arrived back at the Falcon, Luke busied himself in the back bar until opening time, still, eating his sandwich as he unlocked the door for the waiting customers.

Within 30 minutes there was a good trade going and Sally surveyed the group of Luke's friends who crowded around the bar.

" Well. At least you've brought some new trade to the place, Lou."

" Yeh. The best, Sall."

She laughed lightly and moved back into the front bar, throwing Luke a warm smile.

It wasn't long before Dave, Debbie and the crew arrived, together in a loud, laughing band, minus Ruth. They spilled through the doorway and threw themselves onto the bench seats as they joked.

Debbie stood near Dave, looking decidedly off colour.

244

" Hi, Dave. Debs. You don't look too good, girl?"
" I'm okay."

He filled their order, Debbie sipping a coke.

" Lou, can I talk to you?"
" It's a free country, Deb."
" I mean, alone, please."
" I'm a bit pushed right now."
" You always are, aren't you, for some people?"
" Yeh. Guess I is, Debs. Just like you, last night?"
" That's what I want to talk to you about."
" S'okay. I've heard enough about it already, thanks. You can do wot you fuckin well likes with your life, girl, just keep me well out of it from now on. That's twice now you've pissed me about with fella's. Get your real friends to take you about in future."
" But, Lou."
" Listen, Debs, I don't really want to offend you, girl, but just piss off over to your friends before I says somethin that I'll regret. Go back to Trev, like a good little girl, you was all over him last night, yeh?"

He turned away and started to serve another customer, finding Sally eying him from beside the till.

" That was a bit strong, wasn't it, Lou?"

" Not that its none of your business, Sall, but she does have a habit of pissin me off, somewhat."

" But, even so."

" Sall, mind it, will you, girl."

" Well. Sorry I spoke."

"Yeh, me and you both, girl."

She wheeled away and Luke sighed as he lit up another smoke, knowing that he had upset Sally now as well as Debbie.

This just was not working out for Luke as he had hoped it would. Far too many complications were obstructing his progress. Should he leave the Falcon, leave Bromyard again?

London was just as bad, though, with Lydia after his blood, as well as Slim's Daughters, though he still had fond memories of Kirsty now that she had recovered. The same held good for Ireland, though Luke seriously doubted if he would ever be welcome back there with Maire and the family. Possibly even his very life would be in danger now, as he guessed that he had offended Michael and the others in the IRA hierarchy by leaving so suddenly. He still pondered whether or not Con had been involved in the attempted murder of his friends and himself in London, but shook his head as he moved to serve more waiting customers. There was always something waiting to fuck your life up, it seemed.

Debbie was seated next to Carol, but was not responding to her giggling chat. Then, as Luke was talking to Nigel and Phil, Trev burst through the door and stood, grinning over at Dave's group, as full of himself as ever, it seemed.

" Hi folks. I'm here. Iv'e arrived. Come on, let me get you all a refill."

Trev crossed to them, his eyes fixed on Debbie and Phil put his pint down, looking over his shoulder.

" Who the fuck is that arsehole, Lou?"
" Oh. That's Trev. He's a DJ at disco's."
" Yeh? And don't he fuckin well know it. Fuckin arrogant cunt. Pissin ponce that he is."

They were all crowding around Trev now, save for Dave, who was carrying the empties over to the bar for Luke to refill, and Debbie, who was sitting, sad-faced, but listening to him.

Nigel grinned.

" Hey, Lou. You ain't been shit out by Mr fuckin disco man, have you?"

" Naw. But it's beginning to get on me tits all the same."

" Wot, like Crossroads does, you means?"

" Ha. Yeh. Right. C'mon, let's give you cretins a refill."

When Luke looked again, both Trev and Debbie were gone and he wiped the bar top savagely, turning up the juke box as 'Legs' came on.

That night, in bed, Luke gave Sally his very best attention, making love to her tenderly and wholeheartedly long into the early hours.

The next time that Luke saw Debbie was while he was going into the bank. She saw him, hesitated for a few seconds, but didn't stop. Luke's eyes followed her along the pavement until she disapperd around the corner and he thoughtfully carried on into the building, turning matters over in his mind regarding Debbie.

Luke didn't see Debbie again for almost three weeks, then, one evening, she was back in the bar with Dave and her friends and a laughing Trev. Toby and Bett also came in, followed by Colin and Sarah and, a few minutes later, by a hesitant, Sue, whi smiled shyly over at Luke as he winked at her.

" Hi, babe. You looks guilty about somethin?"

" I didn't know if you'd want me in here?"

" Hell. Why not?"

" Well. I don't know."

" C'mon. I'll get the drinks in for you all."

Sue perched herself on one of the bar stools and lit up two smokes, offering one to Luke.

" I haven't seen you lately, Lou?"

" I know, babe. I always seems to be pushed for time. No other reason, babe."

" Good."

" You busy tonight, babe?"

" No, not really. You going to the dance tomorrow, Lou?"

" Dunno."

" I was."

" Oh. Well, we'll see, then, won't we, Sue."

Trev sat with his arm around Debbie's shoulders, but she sat with her hands firmly clasped in her lap, staring down at the table top, a picture of misery or boredom.

Luke couldn't decide which, and didn't care. Or did he?

Sue grabbed his attention once more.

" Want anything putting on the box, besides 'Legs', that is?"

" Naw, that'll do me nicely, girl, cheers."

Sue pressed his number, then selected her own before gliding back onto her stool, pulling her short skirt down carefully.

" Fancy a burn later, Sue?"
" Oh. You bet. Up the Downs, perhaps?"
" Ha. Yeh, perhaps."
" Good. We can listen to the tapes again, can't we?"
" Yeh."

Luke returned her wide, innocent, stare and laughed at her comical expression as she slowly licked her lips and gave a deep, knowing, wink.

The rest of the evening passed quickly enough, Debbie and Trev slipping out together a little before 10.30pm, neither looking at Luke as they passed quickly through the door.

Chapter 7

By the time Luke arrived back at the Falcon it was 3.00am and he awoke five hours later and had a shower and a shave.

He had promised to take Sue and the gang to the dance that night and grinned as he remembered Sue's beautiful body moving beneath his the previous evening.

He felt a lot better afterwards and set about preparing the bar for opening time after he had eaten a hurried breakfast.

Carrying his coffee, Luke turned on the juke box quietly as he worked. With Sally flittering to and fro, between them, they had it all done well in advance.

As she placed a fresh mug of coffee beside him on the bar, Sally smiled.

" Another late night, Lou?"
" Yeh. Somethin like that."
" I don't know where yo get the energy from?"
" Good old Guinness."
" Huh. An Irish aphrodisiac, is it?"

" Jealous?"

" What? You must be joking."

Luke grabbed Sally as she moved away and pulled her to him.

" Lou. Someone might see through the window."

" Down the cellar, then, c'mon."

She followed him down the trapdoor and, within minutes, they were making love against the wall of the spirits cage, Luke gripping the steel mesh with his fingers as they pumped together.

Eventually, they parted and Sally laughed.

" Well. I've never had it up against a wall before."

" Different, ain't it?"

" Hmm. Nice though. I'll have to go and rearrange myself now. Come on, it's almost opening time."

After treating Luke to a long and sensuous kiss, Sally pulled away and preceded him out of the cellar, Luke gazing thoughtfully up her dress as she paused on the top step with a girlish giggle as she threw him a huge smile before disappearing from view.

That night, Luke, Sue and the rest, filed into the dancehall and across to the bar.

The place was quite full, and the music from Trev's speakers belted out at them. He raised his hand in a greeting to Luke, who returned it, noticing that Debbie was sat on the edge of the stage, tapping her feet gently. She was now obviously a DJ's Moll, Luke thought as he inwardly grinned to himself.

As Luke arrived at the bar, Debbie's eyes swept over him before returning to the dance floor, her look unreadable.

Sue danced with Luke and sat on his knee when they arrived back in the bar area.

Luke saw Ruth arrive with Manda and watched as her eyes opened wide in amazement as she spotted Sue on his lap. Then, her gaze travelled to Debbie, then back to Sue, before she moved on to the bar with her group.

Sue grinned.

" Whoops."
" Huh?"
" Lou. The whole town knows about you and Ruth, dear."
" Ha. I only dances with her, sometimes."

" I'm sure you do, Lou. Don't bother to deny it. Anyway, that's history. This, my dear, Lou, is the present."

She fastened her lips to Luke's and probed him long and hungrily with her searching tongue, breaking apart to smile lovingly at him.

Luke lit up two smokes and passed one to Sue, noticing that Debbie's eyes were upon him once again.

The next time that Luke looked, Debbie and Trev were laughing and talking together at the bar.

Trev grinned over at him.

" Want a refill, Lou?"
" Yeh, why not. Cheers."
" And your young lady, too?"

As Trev ordered them, Debbie stood with her back to them all, seeming, to Luke, to be studying the grain of the dark oak bar top.

Trev bought their drinks over to them.

" Not a bad turnout, Lou?"
" Naw. Seems to be a lot here, don't there?"
" Anyway. Must get back."

Sue resettled herself onto his lap as they all chatted, her head resting lightly against Luke's.

Debbie ignored Luke completely now and talked to Trev, or danced with him as the records played.

They almost touched as they all danced on the floor to a slow number. Debbie's eyes stared out over Trev's shoulder, but didn't seem to focus on Luke, and he didn't return her gaze.

Sue pressed herself tightly against him and Luke bent to kiss her ever waiting lips tenderly. She lifted her head to reach him and, as Luke stood back up, she clung fiercely to him, her arms locked tightly around his neck in a loving embrace.

He kissed her deeply, then, lifting her off the floor, he twirled her around several times before replacing her feet on the ground.

" Whoo. I was flying, Lou. What was that whopper for, anyway, Lou?"

" Felt like it."

" Well, hurry up and feel like it again, will you, please?"

" Fancy a walk?"

" Or a drive?"

" Yeh. Okay. C'mon."

The others came too, and, soon, the car was rocking once more as six eager bodies beat in a frenzy of passion inside it.

Sue had informed Luke that she had to be in by 11.30pm as her parents were playing up so, with 2 minutes to spare, Luke said farewell to her at the corner of her road, dropping the rest of them off, one by one as, they too, had all decided to go home early.

Luke was just driving down the Rhea pitch, when he spotted a group walking towards him and stopped, winding down his window.

" Hi mate."
" Hey, Lou."
" Where you lot off?"
" We decided to go up the dance."
" Bit fuckin late, ain't it? C'mon, I'll give you a lift. I've just come from there."
" Good, is it?"
" Yeh, s'okay. Good enough for you lot, anyway."

As they laughingly crowded into the car. Luke gunned the big motor away and was soon back in the dancehall. He decided to have another pint and leaned on the bar quietly smoking by himself.

Suddenly, behind him, an argument started and a body crashed into him. As he turned to investigate, Luke saw a man coming at the fallen victim. The felled man jumped up and swept Luke's pint from the bar top, catching the other a smacking blow to the side of the head. Then, three others materialised, their empty glasses held menacingly. Without thinking, Luke stepped in to help the lone man.

He grabbed one and kicked him savagely, bringing his knee up hard between the others legs in a ball-crushing slam. Smashing him again with his knee, this time beneath the chin, as his victim shot forward.

Another two men joined in and Luke felled them both within a matter of seconds as he swept around, his fists active. As he reached for another, a table was thrown, catching Luke squarely on the back. He dropped to his knees, groaning as the pain shot through him but struggled forward, right into the waiting steel capped boot of another attacker. Luckily, it caught Luke on the shoulder, but still made him wince.

On his feet once more, Luke went for the one who had kicked him, felling him with a serious of kicks and punches.

Then ,as he turned to face the others, he caught sight of a beer glass out of the corner of his eye. It came towards him unavoidably and burst onto his skull with a force that immediately sent Luke deep into unconsciousness.

When he awoke, Luke found that his head and neck were bandaged and he reclosed his eyes as the pain coursed through him.

He tried to sit up, but the whole room swam crazily before him and disappeared as he slipped back into the dark folds of sleep.

When he opened his eyes again, the blurred face above him moved about and became clearer as Luke blinked.

" Ah. Mr Brown. Welcome back to the land of the living.."

" Hi, nurse. Wot's the time?"

"It's. Oh, it's 2.35pm, and it's Sunday afternoon."

" Sunday? Friggin hell."

" Yes, well. Do you feel like a bit of tea?"

" Any coffee?"

" I'll see what I can find for you. Soup, as well?"

" Coffee first, babe. Okay?"

The nurse looked oddly at him then moved away. Looking around the room Luke saw that he was by himself and, as he gazed out of the window, the door opened.

" Mr Brown. You're awake, then?"
" Yeh. Appears so, don't it."

The man walked forward, leaving another to close the door behind them.

Luke instantly recognized them as police officers.

" Inspector, is it?"
" Well. I see that we can skip the preliminaries. Yes. I'm D I Beaver and this is D S Brookes."
" Charmed. Grab a pew, if there's one."
" Thanks. Lou."
" Ah, Lou, is it, this soon? Okay boys, wot the fuck is I supposed to have done?"
" It's about an assault that you made on some people at a dance last Friday."
" Assault? Alleged assault, don't you mean?"
" Okay, an, alleged, assault."
" Look. I stepped in to help this geezer out, he was fuckin well outnumbered by about four to one. Then, half a dozen started and I got clocked with a fuckin glass, here, on me head, see?"
" Yes. Yes. We can see that. The thing is, one of the men is in pretty bad shape, suffering from being

chopped, which is, as you'll agree, one of your favourite little tricks, is it not?"

" I was defendin meself, sunshine. I didn't use a fuckin glass though, did I?"

" No. But you don't have to, do you, Lou?"

" Meanin?"

" Meaning, that you have spent a lot of time at Her Majesty's pleasure for violence, with or without shooters."

" Fuck you, arseholes. I don't believe this."

" That's only what we know about, so, what else don't we know about you?"

" Fuck off, you wanker. I ain't sayin fuck all without me brief."

" That's no attitude to take."

" Look, I've been fuckin well stitched up here, in more ways than one, too. You just piss off until my solicitor arrives. Chase them twats that used the glass, last time I heard, they was classed as offensive weapons. Yet here you is, tryin to stitch me up for usin me hands in a fight. Fuckin piss off."

" How can you have been stitched up?"

" I'll fuckin well tell you once I gets out of here."

" Perhaps I ought to tell you that there is a constable stationed outside of your door."

" Yeh? As if that's goin to stop me."

" More violence, Lou. That's not going to go down too well with the judge, is it?"

Luke was contemplating grabbing the Inspector just as the nurse came back in. She saw the tense faces and stared at the officers.

" Out. Now."

" I'm sorry nurse, we have........."

" You have, to leave right now, or I will report you for harassing a patient of mine. He is too ill to answer any of your questions at present. Well, are you going?"

The two police officers looked at each other and shrugged as they left without uttering another word, Luke knowing that they were still hovering in the corridor.

" Hey. Thanks, nursey. You ought to be my solicitor with an attitude like that."

" Huh. I detest the way that they think they can harass people. Whatever they may, or may not, have done."

" Yeh. Well. The bastards have got it wrong, again. Babe, can you do me a favour?"

" Exactly, what?"

" Can you phone my solicitor and tell him to get his arse over here right away, like, by tonight?"

" But it's Sunday?"

" Yeh. No sweat. I'll give you his home number. Tell him I'll kick his arse if he ain't here by tea time."

" I can't tell a solicitor that."

" If you don't, he won't believe that it's from me."

Luke gave her the telephone number and lay back in his bed, thinking events over in his mind.

The nurse came back, smiling and Luke winked at her as she grinned.

" All done."

" Thanks, babe. Any chance of a fag?"

" What. In here?"

" Can I go out and have one?"

" Funny. You'll get me shot, you know that, don't you. Hang on."

She was back within two minutes and handed the smouldering cigarette to Luke.

" I lit it for you. I hope you don't mind?"

" Baby. I wouldn't mind anythin that you does."

The nurse stared hard at Luke and looked away quickly as his eyes settled on her.

As Luke drew in deeply, he smiled at her.

" Baby. I love every inch of you."

" Please. Someone might hear."

" Okay. I'll wait till we're alone, then."

This time, she actually blushed and busied herself around the room.

She sat gingerly on the edge of Luke's bed and gazed at him.

" Are you really dangerous?"

" Only if I don't like you."

" Oh. I see. You look okay to me."

" Hey, flattery."

" No. I didn't mean like that."

" Baby. That's twice you've blushed now. I didn't think nurses blushed?"

" Oh. Do be quiet, please, Mr Brown."

" Lou. Call me Lou, babe. And, who's you?"

" Hilary. Hilary Benson."

" Mrs?"

" No. Miss, thank you."

" Hmm. Courtin?"

" No."

" How old is you, Hilary?"

" I'm 29."

" Jeez. Still single, too. Wot's up, you too picky, or wot?"

" Actually, I'm far too busy looking after people such as you. Those who are traumatized and confused."

" Oi. I'm your patient. Be nice to me."

" Okay. Shall I fluff up your pillows?"

" Yeh, magic. Cheers."

As Hilary lifted Luke's head gently to rearrange his pillows, Luke put a hand behind her head and brought his lips to hers. She stayed completely still within his grasp for several seconds and stood, gazing down at him when he let her go.

" Are you always this forward, Lou?"

" Well. It helps to break the ice, don't it?"

" Haha. You really are a case, aren't you, Lou. Anyway, I must get on as I'm off soon."

" Hey, babe. You ain't leavin me, is you?"

" My shift finishes at five. But I must get on soon, else Sister will have a fit. I don't like leaving you at the tender mercies of those police though."

" Don't worry, babe. I'll behave now, I promise."

" You'd better, or your Solicitor will have a fit."

" Huh. This place is worse than nick."

" Have you been in prison before, then?"

" Yeh."

" Oh. What for. Oh, please, excuse me. I'm so nosy, forgive me?"

" Yeh, course I will. You're a women, it's only natural, ain't it?"

" Lou."

" Sorry, babe. I went after someone with a shooter."

" A gun?"

" Yeh. Sawn off shotgun."

" My God. You do sound dangerous."

" Sorry to disappoint you, babe."

" You don't look the sort."

" It was a long time ago."

" And you've changed?"

" Naw. Not really, I'm still as big an arsehole as I was then."

" Will you go to prison for this?"

" If I get stitched up I will, yeh."

" What exactly happened, then?"

Luke explained the circumstances and events at the dance and Hilary stared at him, her eyes wide.

" But, Lou. Someone must have seen what happened, surely they will stick up for you?"

" Yeh. Guess so."

" Can I help. Can I see anyone for you?"

" Forget it, babe. Stick to nursing, it's safer. I don't want you to get involved in this shit. Thanks all the same, babe."

" But it's so unfair."
" Yeh. I know."

As the door opened, Hilary jumped up from his bed.

" Oh, hello, Sister."
" Nurse. Can I see you for a minute, please?"

She followed the Sister out of the room and Luke rested his head on the pillows and, feeling the bandage, found that the damage was to his left ear and the rear of his skull. As his hair didn't appear to have been cut off, Luke decided that it wasn't too serious, after all.

Hilary came back in and gathered up some items, including his empty cup and cigarette end.

" I've got to go now, but you're going to be moved tomorrow, by the sound of things. I'll see what else I can find out for you before I go."
" Cheers, baby. I'll remember you."

Hilary smiled at Luke as she left the room and he dozed back off to sleep.

Luke opened his eyes to find the two CID officers there and they turned to him as he yawned.

" Well, Lou. Talkies time."

" Piss off."

" We will, when we're ready. You won't though. You'll be back where you belong, behind bars."

" Go screw your fuckin selves."

" Are you going to answer our questions, or do we do this the long, and hard, way? Make a statement now and you'll be out that much quicker.

" Nothin to say, arsehole."

" Do you deny attacking these men, without provocation, one, by the name of Michael Thompson?"

" Never heard of the wanker. Listen, cuntsworth, you is tryin to stitch me up, and I got nothin more to say."

"As my client has stated, he has nothing to say, officer. May I ask if this is an official interview, or a personal vendetta against Mr Brown? I can assure you that I will be exceedingly clear in my detailed report to your Chief Constable regarding this untoward harassment of Mr Brown"

Luke grinned as his solicitor entered, resplendent in his Saville Row suit.

The DI looked at him and hesitated.

" And, you are, Sir?"

" I, Sir, are Mr Brown's solicitor, Mr Andrew-Templeton-Adams."

" From London?"

" Naturally."

" How the hell did you get here?"

" I think that is my own affair, don't you? Now. Inspector, I take it that you are, at least, an Inspector?"

" Oh. Yes, Sir. I'm D I Beaver."

" How apt. I expect to be speaking to your superiors shortly. I understand that my clients clothes are in your possession, may I ask, why, Inspector?"

" For forensic tests, Sir."

" What type of tests?"

" Due to the case being one of assault."

" Alleged assault, I believe?"

" Yes. Yes, of course. Alleged assault."

" And it was considered necessary to confiscate his clothes, for a mere, alleged, assault charge? On whose authority was this order given, may I enquire?"

The Inspector merely shrugged as Luke's Solicitor went on.

" Indeed, as I thought, a bit of an easy mark for you, am I not correct? No doubt, then, your superiors

268

will be able to furnish me with the relevant information, as I shall demand to see the relevant paperwork regarding this untoward harrassment? Now, please. Carry on with your interrogation, sorry a slip of the tongue, your interview."

The D I shook his head.

" I need to go and make a phone call first."
" A very wise move, Inspector. In the meantime, I will garner the necessasy information from your colleague for my own records so that I can identify you both in my report to your chief. I mean, we do not want any slip-up by laying the guilt at the wrong people, do we, officer?"

Andrew was a very well known solicitor, not only around London, but throughout the country, where his skills were sought after by those that could afford his talents.

Luke had met Andrew all those years before in Bromyard when he went with Andrew's Daughter, Betty and had kept their friendship up, bumping into Andrew one day in London quite by accident while walking through the grounds of Westminster Abbey.

When D I Beaver returned he looked a lot less cocky.

" We'll be leaving now, Sir."

" Is my client under arrest?"

" No, Sir. He's free to go. We will be in touch with him in due course."

" I am sure you will be. Now, officer, I would hate to detain you, so, goodbye."

Luke grinned at the look the officers gave him.

" Well out of your fuckin depth, ain't you, sunshine."

Andrew tutted as the door closed.

" Lou. Please, please refrain from doing that. Anyway, how are you, apart from this spot of bother?"

" Okay. You?"

" Never better. Never better. Betty sends her, ahem, deepest love to you. She also wants to know when you are going to visit her?"

" I'll let you know, Andrew."

" Coward."

" Yup."

" Okay. Let's hear your side of events."

Luke told him, word for word, as he remembered it, and Andrew shook his head.

" They have nothing. You have witnesses, I trust?"

" Yeh, friggin bucketfull's of them."

" Hmm. Good. I don't see a problem here at all, Lou. I will, however, pursue this police harassment theme, as I feel sure that they singled you out solely on your record. Find me a few independent witnesses and it will be all over. I spoke to the Sister earlier. The doctor says that you can go in the morning."

" If I get me clothes back."

" They'll be here, have no fear. If not, I can lend you some of mine.

"Fuckin hell, Andrew, you tryin to make me a laughin stock, fuck that, no thanks."

Andrew gazed over at Luke with a serious frown.

"And what, may I ask, is wrong with my clothes. I think I look rather dapper wearing them?"

"Ha. Nothin at all, mate, for you. For the rest of the planet though, fuckin hell, you looks like a tart."

Andrew looked genuinely shocked for several seconds, then, as he gazed out of the window, a humorous expression crossed his face.

"Point taken, Lou, though I do not look like a tart. So, are you going to contact Betty?"

"Naw, best left well alone I think, Andrew."

"You know, Lou, if I had known about your liaison with Betty, back then, I would have expected a discount on the bikes that I purchased from you."

"Haha, mate, you did get a fuckin discount, I can assure you."

"Really? Thank you, Lou. Now, I will trot off and ensure that your clothes await you. Take care, and keep in touch, with us both, please."

The clothes were ready and waiting for him, and Luke was discharged by 11.30am the following morning, also having the bandages removed. All that remained now was a plaster just behind his left ear, covering where the edge of the glass had caught him.

After taking a taxi home to the Falcon, Luke walked in and explained it all to a worried-looking Sally.

" I've only just heard, Lou. I phoned up the hospital, but they said that you were on your way back. I wondered what had happened to you. Are you okay now?"

" Yeh, no sweat, babe."

" You poor thing."

" Aw. A cup of coffee and a kiss will soon put me right."

" What. In that order?"

" Well, I'll go for the kiss first, if you like."

" I do like, very much."

Sally clung to him for several minutes, her lips fastened tightly to Luke's, as if seeking sanctuary there. Then, breaking, she scurried away to the kitchen, sniffing quietly to herself.

After Luke had finished his coffee and sandwiches, he asked Sally for a lift to the dancehall to pick up his car, then returning to the Falcon, discussed his next moves with Sally.

It took Luke three days to find his independent witnesses, finding, in total, fourteen people willing to come and testify to Luke's innocence in the matter.

Luke phoned Andrew up and was told to leave it all to him, which Luke did, receiving a call from Andrew at the beginning of the following week informing Luke that all charges against him had been dropped, and that Andrew was contacting the Chief Constable direct to demand an answer as to why Luke had been singled out in this way, when, quite obviously, the other parties were to blame, and should be prosecuted.

Sue had continued to come into the Falcon at regular intervals to see Luke and was overjoyed when he told her the news.

She persuaded Luke to take her up the common for the afternoon and, after they had made love, he sat in the passenger seat with her snuggled up to Luke on his lap, listening to one of the Fleetwood Mac tapes.

As she kissed him, Sue smiled.

" I often wonder about all of this, Lou, how many girls you've been with and that?"

" Don't really matter, does it, babe?"

" How many children do you have?"

" A few."

" Don't you know?"

" Yeh. Course I does, babe."

" Do you like children?"

" Yeh, that's why I picked you."

" Lou. That wasn't very nice, was it?"

" Naw. Sorry Sue. Why all the questions, anyway?"

" Because I'm pregnant, Lou."

" Oh, jeez."

Her eyes burned into Luke's.

" Don't worry. I won't burden you with it."

" You ain't gettin rid of it."

" I know I'm not. Anyway, would it matter if I was?"

" Yeh. To the kid, it would. And, me, too."

" Oh. Lou. Don't you mind, then?"

" Sue. I'm chuffed, really fuckin chuffed. But wot will your folks say?"

" Wot can they say? I'm sixteen, after all."

" I'll see you and the babe's okay for money, Sue."

" It's you that I want, not your money, Lou. Not that I'll ever get you, I know that I can't trap you into staying with me because of my child."

" Our child, babe. Remember?"

" Oh, Lou. I love you so very much."

Later that evening, Luke told Sally all about himself and Sue.

" She isn't that tiny girl, Lou, is she, surely, with the long black hair?"

" Yeh, that's her."

" Well. How old is she?"

" Sixteen."

" That's a relief, anyway. I always remember her because of the belts that she wears, that pass as skirts. If the were ant shorter, then she may as not wear any."

" They ain't that short."

" You're a man, Lou, and nothing could be short enough for you lot. Well, this puts a different light on things, doesn't it, Lou?"

" How, Sall?"

" Is she keeping the baby?"

" Yeh, course she is."

" And what about you?"

" I'll pay for its upkeep and make sure that Sue don't go short of dosh."

" That'll cost you thousands."

" Sall. I has thousands, believe me."

" Oh. I see. Well, I don't wish to poke my nose in, Lou. Of course, as you're such a rich, eligible, man, but..."

" Hey. A woman after me own heart."

" No doubt, you won't be staying with her?"

" Doubt it."

" Also, no doubt, you'll be moving on from here soon, too?"

" Let's cross that bridge when we comes to it, shall we, Sall?"

" What happened to Debbie?"

" How do you mean?"

" I haven't seen her lately?"

" S'pect she's with her boyfriend."

" Oh. I see. Enough said."

Luke reached up for Sally, squeezing her arm lightly.

276

" Baby. I think one hell of a lot of you, remember that."

" I'm quite attached to you, as well, Lou, remember that."

Sally stood up then and left Luke a she prepared the bar for opening later.

The end of Chapters Of Life - Luke's Return Book 3

This edition first published in 2019
ISBN: 978-0-244-17632-7
Copyright held by Ed Harris.
No part of this work may be used in any format without the prior
written consent of the author.

www.edharris.co.uk

www.ingramcontent.com/pod-product-compliance
Lightning Source LLC
Chambersburg PA
CBHW052021020726
47501CB00004B/1167